The Hunt Ball Mystery

By Sir William Magnay

Originally published in 1918

The Hunt Ball Mystery

© 2010 Resurrected Press
www.ResurrectedPress.com

Published by Intrepid Ink, LLC

Intrepid Ink, LLC provides full publishing services to authors of fiction and non-fiction books, eBooks and websites. From editing to formatting, to publishing, to marketing, Intrepid Ink gets your creative works into the hands of the people who want to read them.
Find out more at www.IntrepidInk.com.

ISBN 13: 978-1-935774-23-5

Printed in the United States of America

FOREWORD

In The Hunt Ball Mystery Sir William Magnay is writing about a world that he undoubtedly knew very well; the world of fox-hunts, shooting parties, country houses, and lavish parties as it existed before the First World War. It is a world that was forever altered in the trenches of France and for the most part disappeared during the Great Depression and its aftermath.

Both the grandfather and father of Sir William Magnay had been Lord Mayors of London, and his father had been created a baronet, a title that Sir William succeeded to on his father's death. The family had an estate in the county of Surrey, which one imagines is not much different than that which is portrayed in the novel. In his younger years he would have played the part of a country gentleman, indulging in the sporting life, including shooting parties and riding to hounds. He also would have become familiar with the attitudes and prejudices of his neighbors, which he portrays so well in the novel.

While written before the so-called Golden Age of British mysteries, the period between the two world wars, *The Hunt Ball Mystery* exhibits many of the characteristics of the genre. There is the same closed world of both victim and suspects, the amateur sleuth, the misleading clues that throw suspicion on first one suspect and then another. If he had lived another dozen years Magnay might have become as well known as Christie of Sayers.

The Hunt Ball Mystery is both an interesting and entertaining tale and provides an insider's view of a world that is now long disappeared.

About the Author

Sir William Magnay, (1855-1917) was the second Baronet of Magnay, of Postford House in the county of Surrey. His father, who had been the Lord Mayor of London, had been created the first Baronet Magnay in 1844. In addition to *The Hunt Ball Mystery*, Sir William wrote a number of other novels including *A Prince of Lovers* and *The Mystery of the Unicorn*.

Greg Fowlkes
Editor-In-Chief
Resurrected Press
www.ResurrectedPress.com

TABLE OF CONTENTS

1
THE INTRUDER

"I'm afraid it must have gone on in the van, sir."

"Gone on!" Hugh Gifford exclaimed angrily. "But you had no business to send the train on till all the luggage was put out."

"The guard told me that all the luggage for Branchester was out," the porter protested deprecatingly. "You see, sir, the train was nearly twenty minutes late, and in his hurry to get off he must have overlooked your suit-case."

"The very thing I wanted most," the owner returned. "I say, Kelson," he went on, addressing a tall, soldierly man who strolled up, "a nice thing has happened; the train has gone off with my evening clothes."

Kelson whistled. "Are you sure?"

"Quite." Gifford appealed to the porter, who regretfully confirmed the statement.

"That's awkward to-night," Kelson commented with a short laugh of annoyance. "Look here, we'd better interview the station-master, and have your case wired for to the next stop. I am sorry, old fellow, I kept you talking instead of letting you look after your rattle-traps, but I was so glad to see you again after all this long time."

"Thanks, my dear Harry; you've nothing to blame yourself about. It was my own fault being so casual. The nuisance is that if I don't get the suit-case back in time I shan't be able to go with you to-night."

"No," his friend responded; "that would be a blow. And it's going to be a ripping dance. Dick Morriston, who hunts the hounds, is doing the thing top-hole. Now let's see what the worthy and obliging Prior can do for us."

The station-master was prepared to do everything in his power, but that did not extend to altering the times of the trains or shortening the mileage they had to travel. He wired for the suit-case to be put out at Medford, the next stop, some forty miles on, and sent back by the next up-train. "But that," he explained, "is a slow one and is not due here till 9.47. However, I'll send it on directly it arrives, and you should get it by ten o'clock or a few minutes after. You are staying at the *Lion*?"

"Yes."

"Not more than ten or twelve minutes' drive. I'll do my best and there shall be no delay."

The two men thanked him and walked out to the station yard, where a porter waited with the rest of Gifford's luggage.

"There is a gentleman here going to the *Lion*" he said with a rather embarrassed air; "I told him your fly was engaged, sir; but he said perhaps you would let him share it with you."

Kelson looked black. "I like the way some people have of taking things for granted. Cheek, I call it. He had better wait or walk."

"The gentleman said he was in a hurry, sir," the porter observed apologetically.

"No reason why he should squash us up in the fly," Kelson returned. "I'll have a word with the gentleman. Where is he?"

"I think he is in the fly, sir."

"The devil he is! We'll have him out, Hugh. Infernally cool." And he strode off towards the waiting fly.

"Better see what sort of chap he is before you go for him, Harry," Gifford said deprecatingly as he followed. He knew his masterful friend's quick temper, and anticipated a row.

"If you don't mind, this is my fly, sir," Kelson was saying as Gifford reached him.

"The porter told me it was the *Golden Lion* conveyance," a strong, deeply modulated voice replied from the fly.

"And I think he told you it was engaged," Kelson rejoined bluffly.

"I did not quite understand that," the voice of the occupant replied in an even tone. "I am sorry if there has been any misunderstanding; but as I am going to the hotel–"

"That is no reason why you should take our fly," Kelson retorted, his temper rising at the other's coolness. "I must ask you to vacate it at once," he added with heat.

"How many of you are there?" The man leaned forward showing in the doorway a handsome face, dark almost to swarthiness. "Only two? Surely there is no need to turn me out. You don't want to play the dog in the manger. There is room for all three, and I shall be happy to contribute my share of the fare."

"I don't want anything of the sort–"

Kelson was beginning angrily when Gifford intervened pacifically.

"It is all right, Harry. We can squeeze in. The fellow seems more or less a gentleman; don't let's be churlish," he added in an undertone.

"But it is infernal impudence," Kelson protested.

"Yes; but we don't want a row. It is not as though there was another conveyance he could take."

"All right. I suppose we shall have to put up with the brute," Kelson assented grudgingly. "But I hate being bounced like this."

Gifford took a step to the carriage-door. "I think we can all three pack in," he said civilly.

"I'll take the front seat, if you like," the stranger said, without, however, showing much inclination to move.

"Oh, no; stay where you are," Gifford answered. "I fancy I am the smallest of the three; I shall be quite comfortable there. Come along, Harry."

With no very amiable face Kelson got in and took the vacant seat by the stranger. His attitude was not conducive to geniality, and so for a while there was silence. At length as they turned from the station approach on to the main road the stranger spoke. His deep-toned voice had a musical ring in it, yet somehow to Gifford's way of thinking it was detestable. Perhaps it was the speaker's rather aggressive and, to a man, objectionable personality, which made it seem so.

"I am sorry to inconvenience you," he said, more with an air of saying the right thing than from any real touch of regret. "On an occasion like this they ought to provide more conveyances. But country towns are hopeless."

"Oh, it is all right," Gifford responded politely. "The drive is not very long."

"A mile?" The man's musical inflection jarred on Gifford, who began to wonder whether their companion could be a professional singer. One of their own class he certainly was not.

"I presume you gentlemen are going to the Hunt Ball?" he asked.

"Yes," Gifford answered.

"Rather a new departure having it in a private house," the man said. "Quite a sound idea, I have no doubt Morriston will do us as well—much better than we should fare at the local hotel or Assembly Rooms."

"Are you going?" They were the first words Kelson had uttered since the start, and the slight surprise in their tone was not quite complimentary. It must have so struck the other, seeing that he replied with a touch of resentment:

"Yes. Why not?"

"No reason at all," Kelson answered, except that I don't remember to have seen you out with the Cumberbatch."

"I dare say not," the other rejoined easily. "It is some years since I hunted with them. I'm living down in the south now, and when I'm at home usually turn out with the Bavistock. Quite a decent little pack, *faute de mieux*; and Bobby Amphlett, who hunts them, is a great pal of mine."

"I see," Kelson observed guardedly. "Yes, I believe they are quite good as far as they go."

The stranger gave a short laugh. "They, or rather a topping old dog-fox, took us an eleven mile point the other day, which was good enough in that country. Being in town I thought I would run down to this dance for old acquaintance' sake. Dare say one will meet some old friends."

"No doubt," Kelson responded dryly.

"As you have been good enough to ask me to share your fly," the man observed, with a rather aggressive touch of irony, "I may as well let you know who I am. My name is Henshaw, Clement Henshaw."

"Any relation to Gervase Henshaw?" Gifford asked.

"He is my brother. You know him?"

"Only by reputation at my profession, the Bar. And I came across a book of his the other day."

"Ah, yes. Gervase scribbles when he has time. He is by way of being an authority on criminology."

"And is, I should say," Gifford added civilly.

"Yes; he is a smart fellow. Has the brains of the family. I'm all for sport and the open-air life."

"And yet," thought Gifford, glancing at the dark, rather intriguing face opposite to him, "you don't look a sportsman. More a *viveur* than a regular open-air man, more at home in London or Paris than in the stubbles or covert." But he merely nodded acceptance of Henshaw's statement.

"My name is Kelson," the soldier said, supplying an omission due to Henshaw's talk of himself. "I have hunted this country pretty regularly since I left the Service. And my friend is Hugh Gifford."

"Gifford? Did not Wynford Place where we are going to-night belong to the Giffords?" Henshaw asked, curiosity overcoming tact.

"Yes," Gifford answered, "to an uncle of mine. He sold it lately to Morriston."

"Ah; a pity. Fine old place," Henshaw observed casually. "Naturally you know it well."

"I have had very good times there," Gifford answered, with a certain reserve as though disinclined to discuss the subject with a stranger. "I have come down now also for old acquaintance' sake," he added casually.

"I see," Henshaw responded. "Not altogether pleasant, though, to see an old family place in the hands of strangers. Personally, when a thing is irrevocably gone, as, I take it, Wynford Place is, I believe in letting it slide out of one's mind, and having no sentiment about it."

"No doubt a very convenient plan," Gifford replied dryly. "All the same, if I can retrieve my evening kit, which has gone astray, I hope to enjoy myself at Wynford Place to-night without being troubled with undue sentimentality."

"Good," Henshaw responded with what seemed a half-smothered yawn. "Regret for a thing that is gone past recall does not pay; though as long as there is a chance of getting it I believe in never calling oneself beaten. Here we are at the *Lion*."

2
THE STAINED FLOWERS

"What do you think of our acquaintance?" Gifford said as they settled down in the private room of Kelson, who made the *Golden Lion* his hunting quarters.

"Not much. In fact, I took a particular dislike to the fellow. Wrong type of sportsman, eh?"

"Decidedly. Fine figure of a man and good-looking enough, but spoilt by that objectionable, cock-sure manner."

"And I should say a by no means decent character."

"A swanker to the finger-tips. And that implies a liar."

"Not worth discussing," Kelson said. "He goes to-morrow. I made a point of inquiring how long he had engaged his room for. One night."

"Good. Then we shan't be under the ungracious necessity of shaking him off. I can't tell you how sick I am, Harry, at the loss of my things."

"No more than I am, my dear fellow. If only a suit of mine would fit you. But that's hopeless."

They both laughed ruefully at the idea, for Captain Kelson looked nearly twice the size of his friend.

"We'll hope they'll arrive in time for you to see something of the fun at any rate," Kelson said. "I'm in no hurry; I'll wait with you."

"You will do nothing of the sort, Harry," Gifford protested. "Do you think I can't amuse myself for an hour or two alone? You'll go off at the proper time. Absurd to wait till every decent girl's card is full."

"I don't like it, Hugh."

"Nor do I. But it is practically my fault in not looking sharper after my luggage, and better one should suffer than two."

So it was arranged that Captain Kelson should go on alone and his guest should follow as soon as his clothes turned up and he could change into them.

That settled, they sat down to dinner.

"Tell me about the Morristons, Harry," Gifford said. "He is a very good fellow, isn't he?"

"Dick Morriston? One of the best. Straight goer to hounds and straight in every other capacity, I should say. You know they used to live at Friar's Norton, near here, before they bought your uncle's place."

"Yes, I know. What is the sister like?"

"A fine, handsome girl," Kelson answered, without enthusiasm. "Rather too cold and statuesque for my taste, although I have heard she has a bit of the devil in her. Quite a sportswoman, and as good after hounds as her brother. They say she had a thin time of it with her stepmother, and has come out wonderfully since the old lady died. Lord Painswick, who lives near here, is supposed to be very sweet on her. Perhaps the affair will develop to-night. The ball will be rather a toney affair."

"Morriston has plenty of money?"

"Heaps. And the sister is an heiress too. The old man did not nearly live up to his income and there were big accumulations."

"Which enabled the son to buy our property," Gifford said with a tinge of bitterness. "Well, it might have been worse. Wynford has not passed into the hands of some Jew millionaire or City speculator, but has gone to a gentleman, a good fellow and a sportsman, eh?"

"Yes; Dick Morriston is all that. As the place had to go, you could not have found a better man to succeed your people."

When the time came to start for the ball Gifford went down to see his friend off and to repeat his orders concerning the immediate delivery of his suit-case when it should arrive. Henshaw was in the hall, bulking big in a fur coat and complaining in a masterful tone of the unpunctuality of his fly. A handsome fellow, Gifford was constrained to acknowledge, and of a strong, positive character; the type of man, he thought, who could be very fascinating to women—and very brutal.

He dropped his rather bullying manner as he caught sight of the two friends; and, noticing Gifford's morning clothes, made a casually sympathetic remark on his bad luck.

"Oh, I shall come on when my things arrive, which ought to be soon," Gifford responded coldly, disliking the man and his rather obvious insincerity.

"We might have driven over together," Henshaw said, addressing Kelson. "But I hardly cared to propose it after the line you took at the station."

There was an unpleasant curl of the lip as he spoke the words almost vindictively, as though with intent to put Kelson in the wrong.

But his sneer had no effect on the ex-Cavalryman.

"I am driving over in my own trap," he replied coolly, ignoring the other's intent. "You will be a good deal more comfortable in a closed carriage."

"Decidedly," Henshaw returned with a laugh. "I am not so fond of an east wind as to get more of it than can be helped. And, after all, it is best to go independently to an affair of this sort. One may get bored and want to leave early."

Kelson nodded with a grim appreciation of the man's trick of argument, and went out to his waiting dog-cart. Henshaw's fly drove up as Gifford turned back from the door.

"I suppose we shall see you towards midnight," he said lightly as he passed Gifford, his tone clearly suggesting his utter indifference in the matter.

"I dare say," Gifford replied, and as he went upstairs he heard an order given for "Mr. Henshaw's fire in number 9 to be kept up against his return."

Alone in the oak-panelled sitting-room Gifford settled down to wait for his clothes. He skimmed through several picture-papers that were lying about, and then took up a novel. But a restless fit was on him, and he could not settle down to read. He threw aside the book and began thinking of the old property which his uncle had muddled away, and recalling the happy times he had spent there from his schooldays onwards. Memories of the rambling old house and its park crowded upon him. By force of one circumstance or another he had not been there for nearly ten years, and a great impatience to see it again took hold of him. He looked at the clock. At the best, supposing there were no hitch, his suit-case could hardly arrive for another hour and a half. Wynford Place was a bare mile away, perhaps twenty minutes' walk; the night was fine and moonlight, he was getting horribly bored in that room; he would stroll out and have a look at the outside of the old place. After all, it was only the exterior that he could expect to find unaltered; doubtless the Morristons with their wealth had transformed the interior almost out of his knowledge. Anyhow he would see that later. Just then he simply longed for a sight of the ancient house with its detached tower and the familiar landmarks.

Accordingly he filled a pipe, put on a thick overcoat and a golf cap and went out, leaving word of his return within the hour. But it was a good two hours before he reappeared, and the landlord, who met him with the news that the missing suit-case had been awaiting him in his room since twenty minutes past ten, was struck by a certain peculiarity in his manner. It was nothing very much beyond a suggestion of suppressed excitement and that rather wild look which lingers in a man's eyes when he is just fresh from a dispute or has experienced a narrow escape from danger. Then Gifford ordered a stiff glass of spirits and soda and drank it off before going up to change.

"Shall you be going to Wynford Place, sir?" the landlord inquired as he glanced at the clock.

Gifford hesitated a moment. "Yes. Let me have a fly in a quarter of an hour," he answered.

But it was more than double that time when he came down dressed for the dance.

The old house looked picturesque enough in the moonlight as he approached it. All the windows in the main building were lighted up, and there was a pleasant suggestion of revelry about the ivy-clad pile. Standing some dozen yards from the house, but connected with it by a covered way, was a three-storied tower, the remains of a much older house, and from the lower windows of this lights also shone.

Gifford entered the well-remembered hall and made his way, almost in a dream, to the ball-room, where many hunting men in pink made the scene unusually gay. Unable for the moment to catch sight of Kelson, he had to introduce himself to his host, who had heard of his mishap and gave him a cheerily sympathetic welcome. Richard Morriston was a pleasant-looking man of about five or six-and-thirty, the last man, Gifford thought, he would bear a grudge against for possessing the old home of the Giffords.

"I'm afraid you must look upon me rather in the light of an intruder here," Morriston said pleasantly.

"A very acceptable one so far as I am concerned," Gifford responded with something more than empty civility.

"It is very kind of you to say so," his host rejoined. "Anyhow the least I can do is to ask you with all sincerity to make yourself free of the place while you are in the neighbourhood. Edith," he called to a tall, handsome girl who was just passing on a man's arm, "this is Mr. Gifford, who knows Wynford much better than we do."

Miss Morriston left her partner and held out her hand. "We were so sorry to hear of your annoying experience," she said. "These railway people are too stupid. I am so glad you retrieved your luggage in time to come on to us."

Gifford was looking at her with some curiosity during her speech, and quickly came to the conclusion that Kelson's description of her had certainly not erred on the side of exaggeration. She looked divinely handsome in her ball-dress of a darkish shade of blue, relieved by a bunch of roses in her corsage and a single diamond brooch. Statuesque, too statuesque, Kelson had called her; certainly her manner and bearing had a certain cold stateliness, but Gifford had penetration enough to see that behind the reserve and the society tone of her welcome there might easily be a depth of feeling which his friend with a lesser knowledge of human nature never suspected. An interesting girl, decidedly, Gifford concluded as he made a suitable acknowledgment of her greeting, and, I fancy, my friend Harry takes a rather too superficial view of her character, he thought, as strolling off in search of Kelson, he found himself watching his hostess from across the room with more than ordinary interest.

He soon encountered Kelson coming out of a gaily decorated passage which he knew led to the old tower. He had a pretty girl on his arm, tall and fair, but with none of Miss Morriston's dignified coldness. This girl had a sunny, laughing face, and Gifford thought he understood why his friend had not been enthusiastic over the probable Lady Painswick.

Kelson, receiving him with delight, introduced him, with an air of proprietorship it seemed, to his companion, Miss Tredworth.

"Have you been exploring the old tower?" Gifford asked.

"We've been sitting out there," Kelson answered with a laugh. "They have converted the lower rooms into quite snug retreats."

"In my uncle's day they were anything but snug," Gifford observed. "I remember we used to play hide-and-seek up there."

He spoke with preoccupation, his eyes fixed on a bunch of white flowers which the girl wore on her black dress. They were slightly blotched and sprinkled with a dark colour in a way which was certainly not natural, and Gifford, held by the peculiar sight, looked in wonder from the flowers to the girl's face.

"You must give Gifford a dance," Kelson said, breaking up the rather awkward pause.

"I'm afraid my card is full," Miss Tredworth said, holding it up.

Kelson laughed happily. "Then he shall have one of mine."

But Gifford protested. "Indeed I won't rob you, Harry," he declared. "I'm tired, and should be a stupid partner."

"Tired?" Kelson remonstrated. "Why, you have been resting at the *Lion* waiting for your things while we have been dancing our hardest."

"Resting? No; I went out for a walk," Gifford replied.

"The deuce you did! Where did you go to?"

"Oh, nowhere particular," Gifford answered rather evasively. "Just about the town."

3
THE STREAK ON THE CUFF

Hugh Gifford did not stay very long at the dance. He took a mouthful of supper, and then told Kelson that he had a headache and was going to walk back to the *Golden Lion*.

Kelson was distressed. "My dear fellow, coming so late and going so early, it's too bad. This is the best time of the night. I hope the old place with its memories hasn't distressed you."

"Oh, no," was the answer. "But something has upset me. I'll get back and turn in. By the way, I don't see that man Henshaw."

"No," Kelson replied casually; "I haven't seen him lately. But then I've had something better to think about than that ineffable bounder. He was here all right in the early part of the evening. One couldn't see anything else."

"Dancing?"

"More or less. Well, if you will go, old fellow, do make yourself comfortable at the *Lion* and call for anything you fancy. I'm dancing this waltz."

Gifford left the dance and went back to the hotel. He seemed perplexed and worried, so much so that for some time he paced his room restlessly and then, instead of turning in, he went back to the sitting-room, lighted a pipe, and settled himself there to await his friend's return.

It was nearly three o'clock when Kelson came in.

"Why, Hugh!" he exclaimed in surprise. "Still up?"

"I didn't feel like sleeping," Gifford answered, "and if I'm to keep awake I'd rather stay up."

Kelson looked at him curiously. "I hope the visit to your old home hasn't been too much for you," he remarked with the limited sympathy of a strong man whose nerves are not easily affected.

"Oh, no," Gifford assured him. "Although somehow I did feel rather out of it. I have had rather a teasing day, but I shall be all right in the morning, and am looking forward to a run round the scenes of my childhood."

"Good," Kelson responded, relieved to think his friend's visit was not after all going to be as dismal as he had begun to fear. "Well, Hugh," he added gaily. "I have a piece of news for you."

"Not that you are engaged?"

Something, an almost apprehensive touch, in Gifford's tone rather took his friend aback.

"Why not?"

"To Miss—the girl you were dancing with?"

Again Gifford's tone gave a check to Kelson's enthusiasm.

It was with a more serious face that he replied, "Muriel Tredworth, the best girl in England. I hope, my dear Hugh, you are not going to say you don't think so."

"Certainly not," Gifford answered promptly. "I never saw or heard of her before to-night."

Kelson laughed uncomfortably. A man in love and in the flush of acceptance wants something more than a lukewarm reception of the news. "I'm glad to hear it," he responded dryly. "From your tone one might almost imagine that you knew something against Muriel."

"Heaven forbid!" Gifford ejaculated fervently.

"You don't congratulate me," his friend returned with a touch of suspicion.

Gifford forced a laugh. "My dear Harry, you have taken my breath away. You deserve the best wife in the kingdom, and I sincerely hope you have got her," he said, not very convincingly.

His half-heartedness, not too successfully masked, evidently struck Kelson. "One would hardly suppose you thought so," he said in a hurt tone. "I wish," he added warmly, "if there is anything at the back of your words you would speak out. I should hope we are old friends enough for that."

Gifford glanced at the worried face of the big, simple-minded sportsman, more or less a child in his knowledge of the subtleties of human nature, and as he did so his heart smote him.

"We are, and I hope we always shall be," he declared, grasping his hand. "You are making too much of my unfortunate manner to-night, and I'm sorry. With all my heart I congratulate you, and wish you every blessing and all happiness."

There was an unmistakable ring of sincerity in his speech now, and, without going aside to question its motive, as a more penetrating mind might have done, Kelson accepted his friend's congratulations without question.

"Thanks, old fellow," he responded, brightening as he returned the grasp of Gifford's hand. "I was sure of your good wishes. You need not fear I have made a mistake. Muriel is a thorough good sort, and we shall suit each other down to the ground. We've every chance of happiness."

Before Gifford could reply there came a knock at the door. The landlord entered.

"Beg your pardon, captain," he said, "I'm sorry to trouble you, but could you tell me whether they are keeping up the Hunt Ball very late?"

"No, Mr. Dipper," Kelson answered. "It was all over long ago. I was one of the last to come away. We left to the strains of the National Anthem."

Mr. Dipper's face assumed a perplexed expression.

"Thank you, captain," he said. "My reason for asking the question is that Mr. Henshaw, who has a room here, has not come in."

"Not come in?" Kelson repeated. "Too bad to keep you up, Mr. Dipper."

"Well, captain," said the landlord, "you see it is getting on for four o'clock, and we want to lock up. Of course if the ball was going on we should be prepared to keep open all night if necessary. But my drivers told me an hour ago it was over."

"So it was. I wonder"–Kelson turned to Gifford–"what can have become of the egregious Henshaw. I don't think, as I told you in the ball-room, I have seen him since ten o'clock."

Gifford shrugged. "Unless he has come across friends and gone off with them."

"He couldn't well do that without calling here for his things," Kelson objected. "I suppose he did not do that, unknown to you?" he asked the landlord.

"No, captain. His things are all laid out in his room, and the fire kept up as he ordered."

"Then I don't know what has become of him," Kelson returned, manifestly not interested in the subject. "I certainly should not keep open any longer. If Mr. Henshaw turns up at an unreasonable hour, let him wait and get in when he can. Don't you think so, Hugh?"

Gifford nodded. "I think, considering the hour, Mr. Dipper will be quite justified in locking up," he answered.

"Thank you, gentlemen; I will. Goodnight," and the landlord departed.

Kelson turned to a side table and poured out a drink.

"Decent fellow, Dipper, and uniformly obliging," he said. "I certainly don't see why he should be inconvenienced and kept out of his bed by that swanker, who has probably gone off with some pal and hasn't had the decency to leave word to that effect. Bad style of man altogether. Hullo! What's this?"

"What's the matter?"

Gifford crossed to Kelson, who was looking at his shirt-cuff.

"What's this?"

A dark red streak was on the white linen.

"Hanged if it doesn't look like blood," Kelson said, holding it to the light.

Gifford caught his arm and scrutinized the stain.

"It is blood," he said positively.

4
The Missing Guest

Next morning Captain Kelson took his guest for a long drive round the neighbourhood. Before starting he asked the landlord at what time Henshaw had returned.

"He didn't come in at all, captain," Dipper answered in an aggrieved tone. "His fire was kept up all night for nothing."

"I suppose he has been here this morning," Kelson observed casually.

"No," was the prompt reply. "Nothing has been seen or heard of him here since he left last night for the ball."

Kelson whistled. "That looks rather queer, doesn't it, Hugh?"

Gifford nodded. "Very, I should say. What do you make of it?" he asked the landlord.

That worthy spread out his hands in a gesture of helplessness. "It's beyond me, gentlemen. We can none of us make it out. I've never known anything quite like it happen all the years I've been in the business."

"Oh, you'll have an explanation in the course of the morning all right," said Kelson with a smile at the host's worry. "Don't take it too seriously; it isn't worth it. You've got Mr. Henshaw's luggage, which indemnifies you, and he is manifestly a person quite capable of taking care of himself."

Mr. Dipper gave a doubtful jerk of the head. "It is very mysterious all the same."

Kelson laughed as he went off with his friend.

"I'm afraid I can't get up much interest in the doings of the objectionable Henshaw," he remarked lightly as they started off. "Such men as he know what they are about, and are not too punctilious with regard to other people's inconvenience."

"No," Gifford responded quietly. "All the same, his non-appearance is a little mysterious."

Kelson blew away the suggestion of mystery in a short, contemptuous laugh.

"Oh, he is probably up to some devilry with some fool of a girl," he said in an offhand tone. "I know the type of man. They have a keen scent for impressionable women, of whom a fellow of that sort has always half-a-dozen in tow. No doubt that is what he came down here for—a tender adventure. That's the only kind of hunting he is keen on, take my word for it."

"I quite agree with you there," Gifford answered with conviction, and the subject dropped.

When they returned for luncheon they found that nothing had been heard of the *Golden Lion's* missing guest.

"It is rather an extraordinary move of our friend's," Kelson observed with a laugh. "He surely can't be living all this time in his evening clothes. Not but what a man like that would not let a trifle stand in his way if he had some scampish sport in view. No doubt he is up to a dodge or two by way of obviating these little difficulties."

In the afternoon the two friends went up to Wynford Place to call after the dance. Kelson had naturally been much more inclined to drive over to the Tredworths, about seven miles away, in order to settle his betrothal, but Gifford suggested that the duty call should be paid first, and so it was arranged. To Kelson's delight he heard that Muriel Tredworth and her brother were coming over next day to stay with the Morristons for another dance in the neighbourhood and a near meet of the hounds; so he, warming to the Morristons, chatted away in all a lover's high spirits.

"By the way," he said presently, as they sat over tea, "rather an extraordinary thing has happened at the *Golden Lion*."

"What's that?" asked his host.

"Did you notice a man named Henshaw here last night? A big, dark fellow, probably a stranger to you, but by way of being a former follower of the Cumberbatch."

"An old fellow?" Morriston asked.

"Oh, no. About six-and-thirty, I should say; eh, Hugh?"

"Under forty, certainly," Gifford answered.

"Tall and very dark, almost to swarthiness; of course I remember the man."

Morriston exclaimed with sudden recollection. "I introduced him to a partner."

"I noticed the fellow," observed Lord Painswick, who also was calling. "Theatrical sort of chap. What has he done?"

Kelson laughed. "Simply disappeared, that's all."

"Disappeared!" There was a chorus of interest.

"How do you mean?" Morriston asked.

"Left the hotel at nine last night and has never turned up since," Kelson said with an air of telling an amusing story. "Poor Host Dipper is taking it quite tragically, notwithstanding the satisfactory point in the case that the egregious Henshaw's elaborate kit still remains in his unoccupied bedroom."

"Do you mean to say he never came back all night?" Miss Morriston asked.

"Never," Kelson assured her. "Old Dipper came to us, half asleep, at four o'clock to ask whether he was justified in locking up the establishment."

"And nothing has been seen or heard of the man since," Gifford put in.

"That is queer," Morriston said, as though scarcely knowing whether to take it seriously or otherwise. "Now I come to think of it I don't recollect seeing anything of the man after quite the first part of the evening. Did you, Painswick?"

"No, can't say I did," Painswick answered.

"And," observed Kelson, "he was not a man to be easily overlooked when he was on show. I missed him, not altogether disagreeably, after the early dances."

"What is the idea?" Edith Morriston inquired. "Is there any theory to account for his disappearance?"

"No," Kelson answered, "unless a discreditable one. Gone off at a tangent."

"And still in his evening things?" Painswick said with a laugh. "Rather uncomfortable this weather."

"That reminds me," Morriston said with sudden animation, "one of the footmen brought me a fur coat and a soft hat this morning and asked me if they were mine. They had been unclaimed after the dance and he had ascertained that they belonged to none of the men who were staying here. Nor were they mine."

"That is most curious," Kelson said with a mystified air. "Henshaw was wearing a fur coat and soft hat when we saw him in the hall of the *Lion* just before starting. Don't you remember, Hugh?"

"Yes; certainly he was," Gifford answered.

"Then they must be his," Morriston concluded.

"And where is he—without them?" Painswick added with a laugh. "Dead of cold?"

"It is altogether quite mysterious," Morriston observed with a puzzled air. "He can't be here still."

"Hardly," his sister replied. "You know him?" she asked Kelson.

"Quite casually. So far as nearly coming to a rough and tumble with the fellow for his cheek in scoffing our fly at the station constitutes an acquaintance. Gifford acted as peacemaker, and we put up with the fellow's company to the town. But neither of us imbibed a particularly high opinion of the sportsman, did we, Hugh?"

"No," Gifford assented; "his was not a taking character, to men at any rate; and we rather wondered how he came to be going to the Cumberbatch Ball."

"No doubt he got his ticket in the ordinary way," Morriston said.

"It only shows, my dear Dick," his sister observed, "you may quite easily run risks in giving a semi-public dance in your own house."

Morriston laughed. "Oh, come, Edith," he protested, "we need not make too much of it. We don't know for certain that the man was a queer character."

"One finds objectionable swaggerers everywhere," Painswick put in.

"Anyhow," said Kelson, "if this Henshaw was a bad lot he had the decency to efface himself promptly enough. The puzzle is, what on earth has become of him?"

"I don't know, Mr. Gifford," Morriston said as the two friends were leaving, "whether you would care for a ramble over the old place. A man named Piercy has written to me for permission to go over the house; he is, it appears, writing a book on the antiquities of the county. I have asked him to luncheon to-morrow, and we shall be delighted if you and Kelson will join us as a preliminary to a personally conducted tour of the house. Charlie Tredworth and his sister are coming over for a week's stay, so we shall be quite a respectable party."

Naturally Kelson accepted the invitation with alacrity, and Gifford could do no less than fall in with the arrangement.

"Hope you won't mind going over to Wynford," Kelson said as they drove back. "If it is at all painful to you from old associations, I'll make an excuse for you."

Gifford hesitated a moment. "Oh, no," he answered. "I'll come. There is no use in being sentimental about the place going out of our family, and these Morristons are quite the right sort of people to have it. A splendidly thoroughbred type of girl, Miss Morriston."

Kelson laughed. "Oh, yes; a magnificent creature; cut out for a duchess. Only, you know, my dear Hugh, if I married a woman like that I should always be a little afraid of her. A magnificent chatelaine and all that, but too cold for my taste."

"You think there is no deep feeling under the ice of her manner?"

"I don't know," Kelson replied, as though the idea was quite novel to him. "Never got so far as to think of that. I like a girl with whom you can get on without going through the process of thawing her first. And with Edith Morriston I should say it would be a slow process. Anyhow, she is just the girl for Painswick, who is evidently after her."

"I should say that with him the ice is a little below the surface," Gifford ventured.

Kelson laughed. "You've hit it, Hugh. He's easy enough, but scratch him and you come upon a very straight-laced aristocrat. He and the statuesque Edith Morriston are made for one another."

As they entered the *Golden Lion* the landlord met them.

"Well, Mr. Dipper, any news of your missing guest?" Kelson inquired with characteristic cheeriness, ignoring the troubled expression on that worthy's face.

"No, captain; and we can't imagine what has happened to Mr. Henshaw. There are three telegrams come for him, and I have just got one, reply-paid, to ask whether he is staying here."

"And you replied?"

"Went to Hunt Ball 9 last night. Not been here since," Dipper quoted. "It is rather awkward and unpleasant for me, sir," he added uncomfortably.

"Oh, you've no responsibility in the matter," Kelson assured him. "Don't you worry about it, Mr. Dipper. If the man goes out and does not choose to come back, that, beyond the payment of your charges, can be no affair of yours. Isn't that so, Hugh?"

"Certainly," Gifford assented.

Still their host looked anything but satisfied.

"Yes, sir, that's quite right; all the same, we are beginning not to like the look of it. It is very mysterious."

"It is, Mr. Dipper, to say the least of it," Kelson replied. "Still from such opinion as we were able to form of Mr. Henshaw I don't think it worthwhile making much fuss about it. He'll turn up all right and probably call you a fool for your pains."

"I would not worry about it if I were you," Gifford said quietly.

As they turned to go upstairs a telegraph boy came in and handed his message to the landlord, who read it and handed it to Kelson.

"Please wire me without fail directly Mr. Henshaw returns. Gervase Henshaw, 8, Stone Court, Temple, London," Kelson read.

"That's his brother," Gifford observed.

"All right," said Kelson. "Let him worry if he likes. All you have to do, Mr. Dipper, is what he asks you there."

He went upstairs with Gifford, leaving the landlord reperusing the telegram, his plump face dark with misgiving.

5
THE LOCKED ROOM

That night the missing man did not return, nor was anything heard of him. The morning brought no news, and even Kelson began to think there might be something serious in it.

"If it was anybody but that man," he said casually over a hearty breakfast, "I should say it would be worth while taking steps to find out what had become of him. But that fellow can take care of himself; and when you come to think of it, his coming down here, an outsider, to the ball, was in itself rather fishy."

Gifford agreed, and they fell to discussing the day's plans. Kelson was going to drive over to have the momentous interview with Miss Tredworth's father. He anticipated no difficulty there; still, as he said, "The thing has got to be done, and the sooner it is over the better."

"Why not go to-morrow?" Gifford suggested. "There will be rather a rush to-day."

Kelson, a man of action, scoffed at the idea. "Oh, no; Muriel and Charlie are coming over to Wynford to luncheon. I shall simply get the thing settled and drive back with them."

So it was arranged. Gifford spent the morning in a stroll about the familiar neighbourhood, and when luncheon time came they all met at Wynford Place. Miss Morriston was not present. Her brother apologized for her absence, saying she had been obliged to keep an engagement to lunch with a friend, but that she had promised to return quite early in the afternoon. Mr. Piercy, the antiquarian, proved to be by no means as dry as his pursuit suggested. He was a lively little man with a fund of interesting stories furnished by the lighter side of his work, and altogether the luncheon was quite amusing.

When it was over Morriston suggested that, not to waste the daylight, they should begin their tour of the house; he called upon Gifford to share the duties of guidance, and the party moved off.

"Hope you haven't been bored all the morning, Hugh," Kelson said to his friend as they found themselves side by side. "Any news at the *Lion*? Has Henshaw turned up yet?"

Gifford shook his head. "No. Host Dipper has had another telegram of inquiry from the brother, but had nothing to tell him in return."

Kelson's face became grave. "It really does begin to look serious," he remarked.

"Yes; Dipper has been interviewing the police on the subject."

"Has he? Well, I only hope Henshaw has not been playing the fool, or worse, and caused all this fuss for nothing."

The party moved on to the great hall where the dancing had taken place, and so to the passage connecting the main building with the ancient tower.

"Now this is the part which will no doubt interest you most, Mr. Piercy," Morriston said; "this fourteenth century tower, which is to-day in a really wonderful state of preservation."

"Ah, yes," the archaeologist murmured; "they could build in those days."

They examined the two lower rooms on the ground and first floors, remarked on the thickness of the walls, shown by the depth of the window embrasures, which in older days had been put to sterner purposes; they admired the solid strength of the ties and hammer-beams in the roofs, and scrutinized the few articles of ancient furniture and tapestry the rooms contained, and the massive oaken iron-bound door which admitted to the garden.

"Now we will go up to the top room," Morriston proposed. "It is used only for lumber, but there is quite a good view from it."

He preceded the rest of the party up the winding stairs to the topmost door.

"Hullo!" he exclaimed, pushing at it, "the door is locked. And the key appears to have been taken away," he added, bending down and feeling about in the imperfect light.

The whole party was consequently held up on the narrow stairs. "I'll go and ask what has become of the key," Morriston said, making his way past them.

In a minute he returned, presently followed by the butler.

"How is it that this top door is locked, Stent?" he asked. "And where is the key?"

"I don't know, sir. Alfred mentioned this morning that the door was locked and the key taken away; we thought you must have locked it, sir."

"I? No, I've not been up here since the morning of the ball, when I had those old things brought up from the lower room to be out of the way."

"Did you lock the door then, sir?"

"No. Why should I? I am certain I did not. Perhaps one of the men did. Just go and inquire. And have the key looked for."

"Very good, sir."

"This is rather provoking," Morriston said, as they waited. "I particularly wanted to show you the view, which should be lovely on a clear day like this. If we have to wait much longer the light will be going. Besides, it is quite a quaint old room with a curious recess formed by the bartizan you may have noticed from outside."

Presently the butler returned accompanied by a footman with several keys.

"We can't find the right key, sir," he announced. "No one seems to have seen it. Alfred has brought a few like it, thinking one might possibly fit."

None of them, however, would go into the lock, not even the smallest of them.

"I can't make it out, sir," said the man, kneeling to get more effectively to work. But no key would enter. The footman at last took a box of matches from his pocket, struck a light and, holding it to the key-hole, peered in.

"Why, the key is in the lock, on the other side, sir," he said in astonishment.

"Then the door can't be locked," Morriston said, pushing it.

The footman rose and pushed too, but the door showed no sign of yielding; it was fastened sure enough.

"This is strange," Morriston said. "Hi! Is anyone in there?" he shouted; but no response came.

"Are you sure the key is in the door on the inside?" he asked.

"Certain, sir. Will you look for yourself, sir?" the man replied, striking another match and holding it so that his master could convince himself.

"No doubt about that," Morriston declared, as he rose from his scrutiny. "It is the most extraordinary thing I have ever known. Can you account for it, Stent?"

The butler shook his head. "No, sir. Unless someone is in there now."

Morriston again shouted, but no answer came.

"I presume there is no way out of the room but this door," Piercy asked.

"None," Morriston answered; "except the window, and that is, I should say, quite eighty feet from the ground; eh, Mr. Gifford?"

"A sheer drop of quite that distance," he answered.

"A prohibitive mode of exit," Piercy observed with a smile.

"Yes," Morriston said. "I can't understand it at all. Besides, who would be likely to want to play tricks here?

We have had no sign of burglars, and in any case they would hardly have been able to bring a ladder long enough to reach up to that window. Well, we must have the mystery cleared up. I think, Stent, you had better send one of the men on a bicycle into Branchester to fetch a locksmith and have the door opened somehow. Have it explained to him that it may be a tough job. In the meantime we may as well go and view the tower from the outside, as we can't get in."

Accordingly the whole party went down into the hall and so out to the garden, where they strolled round the house, Piercy meanwhile taking notes of its architectural features. As they came to the tower the rays of a late winter sun were striking it almost horizontally, lighting it up in a picturesque glow. Piercy, with his archaeological knowledge, was able to tell the owner and Gifford a good deal about the ancient structure of which they had previously been ignorant.

"The sunset would have been worth seeing from that top window," Morriston said, evidently perplexed and annoyed over the mystery of the locked door. "I can't make out what has happened."

"The person who locked the door assuredly did not make his exit by the window," Kelson remarked with a laugh, as he looked up at the sheer surface of the upper wall; "unless he was bent on suicide, in which case we should have found what was left of him at the foot of the tower."

As they went on round the house, Miss Morriston was seen coming up the drive. Her brother hurried forward to meet her.

"I say, Edith," he exclaimed, "we are in a great fix. Can you explain how the door of the top room in the tower comes to be locked with the key inside?"

Miss Morriston looked surprised. "What, Dick?"

"We can't get in," Morriston explained. "We found the door locked and the key missing, and then when Alfred tried another key, he found the right one was in the lock but inside the room."

Miss Morriston thought a moment. "My dear Dick, the door can't be locked."

"It is, I tell you," he returned; "most certainly locked. We have tried it and found it quite fast."

"Then there must be someone in the room," his sister said.

"That," Morriston replied, "seems the only possible explanation. But I shouted several times and got no answer."

"Someone playing you a trick," and the girl laughed.

"But who? Who?" he returned.

His sister gave a shrug. "Oh, you'll find out soon enough," she replied, with a smile.

"I shall," he replied, as two men appeared making for the servants' entrance. "Here comes Henry with the locksmith."

Miss Morriston in her stately way looked amused.

"My dear old Dick, you have been making a fuss about it. You will probably find the door open when you go up."

"And I'll know who has been playing this stupid trick," Morriston said wrathfully.

"A footman making love to a housemaid turned the key in a panic at being trapped," Kelson said to his host.

"I dare say," Morriston replied with a laugh of ill-humour. "And he'll have to pay for his impudence."

That explanation by its feasibility was generally accepted as the simple solution of the mystery.

"Come along!" Morriston called. "We'll all go up, and see whether the door is open or not. We shall just be in time to catch the sunset."

He led the way through the hall and the corridor beyond and so up the winding stairs.

"What, not open yet?" he exclaimed as the last turn showed the workman busy at the lock. "Well, this is extraordinary."

The locksmith was kneeling and working at the door, while the footman stood over him holding a candle.

"The key is in the lock, inside, isn't it?" Morriston asked.

"Yes, sir," the man answered. "There is no doubt about that."

"How do you account for it?"

The man looked up from his task and shook his head.

"Can't account for it, sir. Unless so be as there is someone inside."

"Can you open it?"

"Yes, sir. I'll have it turned in a minute."

He took from his bag a long pair of hollow pliers which he inserted in the lock and then screwed tightly, clutching the end of the key. Then fitting a transverse rod to the pliers and using it as a lever he carefully forced the key round, and so shot back the lock.

There was a short pause while the man unscrewed his instrument; then he stepped back and pushed open the door.

Morriston went in quickly. "There is the key, sure enough," he said, looking round at the inside of the door. He took a couple of steps farther into the room, only to utter an exclamation of intense surprise and horror; then turned quickly with an almost scared face.

"Go back!" he cried hoarsely, holding up his hands with an arresting gesture. "Kelson, Mr. Gifford, come here a moment and shut the door. Look!" he said in a breathless whisper, pointing to the floor beneath the window through which the deep orange light of the declining sun was streaming.

An exclamation came from Kelson as he saw the object which Morriston indicated, and he turned with a stupefied look to Gifford. "My–!"

Gifford's teeth were set and he fell a step backward as though in repulsion. On the floor between the window and an old oak table which had practically hidden it from the doorway, lay the body of a man in evening clothes, one side of his shirt-front stained a dark colour. Although the face lay in the shadow of the high window-sill, there was no mistaking the man's identity.

"Henshaw!" Kelson gasped.

6
THE MYSTERY OF CLEMENT HENSHAW

It was the missing man, Henshaw, sure enough. The swarthy hue of his face had in death turned almost to black, but the features, together with the man's big, muscular figure were unmistakable. For some moments the three men stood looking at the body in something like bewilderment, scarcely realizing that so terrible a tragedy had been enacted in that place, amid those surroundings.

"Suicide?" Kelson was the first to break the silence.

"Must have been," Morriston responded "or how could the door have been locked from the inside. I will send at once for the police, and we must have a doctor, although that is obviously useless." He went to the door, then turned. "Will you stay here or—"

Kelson made an irresolute movement as though wavering between the implied invitation to quit the room and an inclination not to run away from the grim business. He glanced at Gifford, who showed no sign of moving.

"Just as you like," he replied in a hushed voice. "Perhaps we had better stay here till you come back."

"All right," Morriston assented. "Don't let anyone come in, and I suppose we ought not to move anything in the room till the police have seen it."

He went out, closing the door.

"I can't make this out, Hugh," Kelson said, pulling himself together and moving to the opposite side of the room.

"No," Gifford responded mechanically.

"He," Kelson continued, "certainly did not give one the idea of a man who had come down here to make away with himself."

"On the contrary," his friend murmured in the same preoccupied tone.

"What do you think? How can you account for it?" Kelson demanded, as appealing to the other's greater knowledge of the world.

It seemed to be with an effort that Gifford released himself from the fascination that held his gaze to the tragedy. "It is an absolute mystery," he replied, moving to where his friend stood.

"A woman in it?"

For a moment Gifford did not answer. Then he said, "No doubt about it, I should imagine."

"It's awful," Kelson said, driven, perhaps for the first time in his life, from his habitually casual way of regarding serious things, and maybe roused by Gifford's apathy. "We didn't like—the man did not appeal to us; but to die like this. It's horrible. And I dare say it happened while the dance was in full swing down there. Why, man, Muriel and I were in the room below. I proposed to her there. And all the time this was just above us."

"It is horrible; one doesn't like to think of it," Gifford said reticently.

"I cannot understand it," Kelson went on, with a sharp gesture of perplexity. "I can imagine some sort of love affair bringing the poor fellow down to this place; but that he should come up here and do this thing, even if it went wrong, is more than I can conceive. Taking the man as we knew him it is out of all reason."

"Yes," Gifford assented. "But we don't know yet that it is a case of suicide."

"What else?" Kelson returned. "How otherwise could the door have been locked. Unless—" He glanced sharply at the deep recess, or inner chamber, formed by the bartizan, hesitated a moment, and then going quickly to it, looked in.

"No, nothing there," he announced with a breath of relief. "I had for the moment an idea it might have been a double tragedy," he added with a shudder.

"So we are forced back to the suicide theory," Gifford remarked. He had gone to the landing outside the door.

"Yes," Kelson replied as he joined him. "But as to the woman in the case, who could she possibly have been? I knew most of the girls who were at the dance, and the idea of a tragedy with any one of them seems inconceivable."

"One would think so," Gifford responded. "And yet—"

"You think it possible?" Kelson demanded incredulously.

"Possible, if far from probable," the other answered with conviction. "There are women who can be as secret as the grave, at any rate so far as appearances to the outer world are concerned. I wonder whom he danced with. Do you remember?"

"No. I seem to recollect him with a girl in a light green dress, but that does not take us far."

Footsteps on the stairway announced their host's return.

"The police will be here, directly," he reported, "and, I hope, a doctor. I have done my best to keep it from the ladies, and I don't think that, so far, any of them has an exact idea of what made me turn them back. Just as well the horror should be kept dark as long as possible. It is such an awful blow to me that I can scarcely realize it yet."

"Miss Morriston does not know?" Kelson asked.

"No. And I only hope it won't give her a dislike to the house when she does. For I am hoping to have her here a good deal with me, even if she marries."

A police inspector accompanied by a detective and a constable now arrived. Morriston took them into the room of death. Gifford grasped Kelson's arm.

"I don't think there is any use in our staying here," he suggested. "Let us go down."

The other man nodded, and they began to descend.

"You are not going, Kelson?" Morriston cried, hurrying to the door.

"We thought we could be of no use and might be in the way," Gifford replied.

"Oh, I wish you would stay," Morriston urged, going down a few steps to them. "I know it is not pleasant; on the contrary it's a ghastly affair; but I should like to have you with me till this police business is over. I won't ask you to stay up here, but if you don't mind waiting downstairs I should be so grateful. I might want your advice. You'll find the rest of the party in the drawing-room."

The two could do no less than promise, and, with a word of thanks, Morriston went back to the officials.

As the two men crossed the hall the drawing-room door opened and Miss Morriston came out.

"Is my brother coming?" she asked.

"He will be down soon," Gifford answered in as casual a tone as he could assume.

The girl seemed struck by the gravity of their faces as she glanced from one to the other. "I hope nothing is wrong," she observed, with just a shade of apprehension.

There was a momentary pause as each man, hesitating between a direct falsehood, the truth, and a plausible excuse, rather waited for the other to speak.

Gifford answered. "No, nothing that you need worry about, Miss Morriston. Your brother will tell you later on."

But the hesitation seemed to have aroused the girl's suspicions. "Do tell me now," she said, with just a tremor of anxiety underlying the characteristic coldness of her tone. "Unless," she added, "it is something not exactly proper for me to hear."

Kelson quickly availed himself of the loophole she gave him. "You had better wait and hear it from Dick," he said, suggesting a move towards the drawing-room. "In the meantime there is nothing you need be alarmed about."

"It all sounds very mysterious," Miss Morriston returned, her apprehension scarcely hidden by a forced smile. "I must go and ask Dick—"

As she turned towards the passage leading to the tower Kelson sprang forward and intercepted her. "No, no, Miss Morriston," he remonstrated with a prohibiting gesture, "don't go up there now. Take my word for it you had better not. Dick will be down directly to explain what is wrong."

For a few moments her eyes rested on him searchingly.

"Very well," she said at length. "If you say I ought not to go, I won't. But you don't lessen my anxiety to know what has happened."

"There is no particular cause for anxiety on your part," Kelson said reassuringly.

She had turned and now led the way to the drawing-room. As they entered they were received by expectant looks.

"Well, is the mystery solved?" young Tredworth inquired.

Kelson gave him a silencing look. "You'll hear all about it in good time," he replied between lightness and gravity.

Piercy rose to take his leave.

"Oh, you must not go yet," Miss Morriston protested. "They are just bringing tea."

"But I fear I may be in the way if there is anything—" he urged.

"Oh, no," his hostess insisted. "I don't know of anything wrong. At least neither Captain Kelson nor Mr. Gifford will admit anything. You must have tea before your long drive."

The subject of the mystery in the tower was tacitly dropped, perhaps from a vague feeling that it was best not alluded to, at any rate by the ladies, and the conversation flowed, with more or less effort, on ordinary local topics. Tea over, Piercy took his leave.

"You must come again, Mr. Piercy, while you are in this part of the county," Miss Morriston said graciously, "when you shall have no episodes of lost keys to hinder your researches. My brother shall write to you."

Kelson took the departing visitor out into the hall to see him off.

"You'll see it all in the papers to-morrow, I expect," he said in a confidential tone, "so there is no harm in telling you there has been a most gruesome discovery in that locked room. A man who was here at the Hunt Ball, has been found dead; suicide no doubt. The police are here now."

"Good heavens! A mercy the ladies did not see it."

"Yes; they'll have to know sooner or later. The later the better."

"Yes, indeed. Any idea of the cause of the sad business?"

"None, as yet. A complete mystery."

"Probably a woman in it."

"Not unlikely. Good-bye."

As Kelson turned from the door, Morriston and another man appeared at the farther end of the hall and called to him.

"You know Dr. Page," he said as Kelson joined them.

"A terrible business this, doctor," Kelson observed as they shook hands.

The medico drew in a breath. "And at first sight in the highest degree mysterious," he said gravely.

"Dr. Page," said Morriston, "has made a cursory examination of the body. The autopsy will take place elsewhere. The police are making notes of everything important, and after dark will remove the body quietly by the tower door. So I hope the ladies will know nothing of the tragedy just yet."

As they were speaking a footman had opened the hall-door and now approached with a card on a salver. "Can you see this gentleman, sir?" he said.

Morriston took the card, and as he glanced at it an expression of pain crossed his face. He handed it silently to Kelson, who gave it back with a grave nod. It was the card of "Mr. Gervase Henshaw, II Stone Court, Temple, E.G."

7

THE INCREDULITY OF GERVASE HENSHAW

"Show Mr. Henshaw into the library," Morriston said to the footman. "This is horribly tragic," he added in a low tone to Kelson, "but it has to be gone through, and perhaps the sooner the better. His brother?"

"Yes; he mentioned him on our way from the station the other evening. At any rate he will be able to see the situation for himself."

"You will come with me?" Morriston suggested. "You might fetch your friend, Gifford."

Kelson nodded, opened the drawing-room door and called Gifford out, while Morriston waited in the hall.

"The brother has turned up," he said as the two men joined him. "No doubt to make inquiries. What are we to say to him?"

"There is nothing to be said but the bare, inevitable truth," Gifford answered. "You can't now break it to him by degrees."

Morriston led the way to the library. By the fire stood a keen-featured, sharp-eyed man of middle height and lithe figure, whose manner and first movements as the door opened showed alertness and energy of character. There was a certain likeness to his brother in the features and dark complexion as well as in a suggestion of unpleasant aggressiveness in the expression of his face, but where the dead man's personality had suggested determination overlaid with an easy-going, indulgent spirit of hedonism this man seemed to bristle with a restless mental activity, to be all brain; one whose pleasures lay manifestly on the intellectual side. One thing Gifford quickly noted, as he looked at the man with a painful curiosity, was that the face before him lacked

much of the suggestion of evil which in the brother he
had found so repellent. This man could surely be hard
enough on occasion, the strong jaw and a certain
hardness in the eyes told that, but except perhaps for an
uncomfortable excess of sharpness, there was none of his
brother's rather brutally scoffing cast of expression.

Henshaw seemed to regard the two men following
Morriston into the room with a certain apprehensive
surprise.

"I hope you will pardon my troubling you like this," he
said to Morriston, speaking in a quick, decided tone, "but
I have been rather anxious as to what has become of my
brother, of whom I can get no news. He came down to the
Cumberbatch Hunt Ball, which I understand was held in
this house, and from that evening seems to have
mysteriously disappeared. He had an important business
engagement for the next day, Wednesday, which he failed
to keep, and this may mean a considerable loss to him.
Can you throw any light on his movements down here?"

Morriston, dreading to break the news abruptly, had
not interrupted his questions.

"I am sorry to say I can," he now answered in a
subdued tone.

"Sorry?" Henshaw caught up the word quickly. "What
do you mean? Has he met with an accident?"

"Worse   than   that,"   Morriston   answered
sympathetically.

Henshaw with a start fell back a step.

"Worse," he repeated. "You don't mean to say–"

"He is dead."

"Dead!" Surprise and shock raised the word almost to
a shout. "You–"

"We have," Morriston said quietly, "only discovered
the terrible truth within the last hour or so."

"But dead?" Henshaw protested incredulously. "How–
how can he be dead? How did he die? An accident?"

"I am afraid it looks as though by his own hand,"
Morriston answered in a hushed voice.

The expression of incredulity on Henshaw's face manifestly deepened. "By his own hand?" he echoed. "Suicide? Clement commit suicide? Impossible! Inconceivable!"

"One would think so indeed," Morriston replied with sympathy. "May I tell you the facts, so far as we know them?"

"If you please," The words were rapped out almost peremptorily.

Morriston pointed to a chair, but his visitor, in his preoccupation, seemed to take no notice of the gesture, continuing to stand restlessly, in an attitude of strained attention.

The other three men had seated themselves. Morriston without further preface related the story of the locked door in the tower and of the subsequent discovery when it had been opened. Henshaw heard him to the end in what seemed a mood of hardly restrained, somewhat resentful impatience.

"I don't understand it at all," he said when the story was finished.

"Nor do any of us," Morriston returned promptly. "The whole affair is as mysterious as it is lamentable. Still it appears to be clearly a case of suicide."

"Suicide!" Henshaw echoed with a certain scornful incredulity. "Why suicide? In connection with my brother the idea seems utterly preposterous."

"The door locked on the inside," Morriston suggested.

"That, I grant you, is at first sight mysterious enough," Henshaw returned, his keen eyes fixed on Morriston. "But even that does not reconcile me to the monstrous improbability of my brother, Clement, taking his own life. I knew him too well to admit that."

"Unfortunately," Morriston replied, sympathetically restraining any approach to an argumentative tone, "your brother was practically a stranger to me, and to us all. My friends here, Captain Kelson and Mr. Gifford, met him casually at the railway station and drove with him to the *Golden Lion* in the town, where they all put up."

Henshaw's sharp scrutiny was immediately transferred from Morriston to his companions.

"Can you, gentlemen, throw any light on the matter?" he asked sharply.

"None at all, I am sorry to say," Kelson answered readily. "I may as well tell you how our very slight acquaintance with him came about."

"If you please," Henshaw responded, in a tone more of command than request.

Kelson, naturally ignoring his questioner's slightly offensive manner, thereupon related the circumstances of the encounter at the station-yard and of the subsequent drive to the town, merely softening the detail of their preliminary altercation. Henshaw listened alertly intent, it seemed, to seize upon any point which did not satisfy him.

"That was all you saw of my unfortunate brother?" he demanded at the end.

"We saw him for a few moments in the hall of the hotel just as we were starting," Kelson answered.

"You drove here together? No?"

"No; your brother took an hotel carriage, and I drove in my own trap."

"With Mr. —?" he indicated Gifford, who up to this point had not spoken.

"No," Gifford answered. "I came on later. A suit-case with my evening things had gone astray–been carried on in the train, and I had to wait till it was returned."

Henshaw stared at him for a moment sharply as though the statement had about it something vaguely suspicious, seemed about to put another question, checked himself, and turned about with a gesture of perplexity.

"I don't understand it at all," he muttered. Then suddenly facing round again he said sharply to Gifford,

"Have you anything to add, sir, to what your friend has told me?"

"I can say nothing more," Gifford answered.

Henshaw turned away again, and seemed as though but half satisfied.

"The facts," he said in a lawyer-like tone, "don't appear to lead us far. But when ascertained facts stop short they may be supplemented. Apart from what is actually known–I ask this as the dead man's only brother–have either of you gentlemen formed any idea as to how he came by his death?"

He was looking at Morriston, his cross-examining manner now softened by the human touch.

"It has not occurred to me to look beyond what seems the obvious explanation of suicide," Morriston answered frankly.

Henshaw turned to Kelson. "And you, sir; have you any idea beyond the known facts?"

"None," was the answer, "except that he took his own life. The door locked on–"

Henshaw interrupted him sharply. "Now you are getting back to the facts, Captain Kelson. I tell you the idea of my brother Clement taking his own life is to me absolutely inconceivable. Have you any idea, however far-fetched, as to what really may have happened?"

Kelson shook his head. "None. Except I must say he looked to me the last man who would do such an act."

"I should think so," Henshaw returned decidedly. Then he addressed himself to Gifford. "I must ask you, sir, the same question."

"And I can give you no more satisfactory answer," Gifford said.

"As a man with knowledge of the world as I take you to be?" Henshaw urged keenly.

"No."

"At least you agree with your friend here, that my poor brother did not strike one as being a man liable to make away with himself?"

"Certainly. But one can never tell. I knew nothing of him or his affairs."

"But I did," Henshaw retorted vehemently. "And I tell you, gentlemen, the thing is utterly impossible. But we shall see. The body—is it here?"

"The police have charge of it in the room where he was found. It is to be removed at nightfall. You will wish to see it?" Morriston answered.

"Yes."

Morriston led the way to the tower, explaining as he went the arrangements on the night of the ball. Henshaw spoke little, his mood seemed dissatisfied and resentful, but his sharp eyes seemed to take everything in. Once he asked, "Did my brother dance much?"

"He was introduced to a partner," Morriston replied. "But after that no one seems to have noticed him in the ball-room."

"You mean he disappeared quite early in the evening?"

"Yes; so far as we have been able to ascertain," Morriston answered. "Naturally, before this awful discovery we had been much exercised by his mysterious disappearance and failure to return to the hotel."

"All the same," Henshaw returned sourly, "one can hardly accept the inference that he came down here for the express purpose of making away with himself in your house."

"No, I cannot understand it," Morriston replied, as he turned and began to ascend the winding stairway.

On the threshold of the topmost floor he paused.

"This is the door we found locked on the inside," he observed quietly.

Henshaw gave a keen look round, and nodded. Morriston pushed open the door and they entered.

The body of Clement Henshaw still lay on the floor in charge of the detective and the inspector, the third man having been despatched to the town to make arrangements for its removal. With a nod to the officials, Henshaw advanced to the body and bent over it. "Poor Clement!" he murmured.

After a few moments' scrutiny, Henshaw turned to the officers. "I am the brother of the deceased," he said, addressing more particularly the detective. "What do you make of this?"

The question was put in the same sharp, business-like tone which had characterized his utterances in the library.

"Judging by the door being locked on the inside," the detective answered sympathetically, "it can only be a case of suicide."

Henshaw frowned. "It will take a good deal to persuade me of that," he retorted. "Mr. —"

"Detective-Sergeant Finch."

"Mr. Finch. Did the doctor say suicide?"

"I did not hear him express a definite opinion. Did you, inspector?"

"No, Mr. Finch. I rather presumed the doctor took it for granted."

"Took it for granted!" Henshaw echoed contemptuously. "I'm not going to take it for granted, I can tell you. Did the doctor examine the body?"

"He made a cursory examination. He is arranging to meet the police surgeon for an autopsy to-morrow morning."

On the table lay a narrow-bladed chisel, the lower portion of the bright steel discoloured with the dark stain of blood.

The inspector pointed to it.

"That is the instrument with which the wound must have been made," he remarked in a subdued tone. "It was found lying beside the body."

Henshaw took it up and ran his eyes over it. "How could he have got this?" he demanded, looking round with what seemed a distrustful glance.

"I can only suggest," Morriston answered, "that one of my men must have left it when some work was done here a few days ago."

"That is so apparently, Mr. Morriston," the detective corroborated. "It has been identified by Haynes, the estate carpenter."

Henshaw put down the chisel and for some moments kept silence, tightening his thin lips as though in strenuous thought. Then suddenly he demanded, "Beyond the fact that the door was found locked from within, what reason have you for your conclusion?"

Mr. Finch shrugged. "We don't see how it could be otherwise, sir," he replied with quiet conviction. "Clearly the deceased gentleman must have been alone in the room when he died."

"Might he not have locked the door after the wound was given?" Henshaw suggested in a tone of cross-examination.

"Dr. Page was of opinion that death, or at any rate unconsciousness, must have been almost instantaneous," Finch rejoined respectfully.

"Even supposing the autopsy bears out that view I shall not be satisfied," Henshaw declared.

The inspector took up the argument.

"You see, sir, taking into consideration the position of the room it would be impossible for any second party who may have been here with the deceased to leave it undiscovered except by the door. To drop from this window, which is the only one large enough to admit of an adult body passing through, would mean pretty certain death. Anyhow the party would have been so injured that getting clear away would be out of the question. Will you see for yourself, sir?"

He threw back the window and invited Henshaw to look down. The argument seemed conclusive.

"Was the window found open or shut?"

"It was found unlatched, sir," Finch answered. "But the servants think that it was opened that morning and owing to the extra work in the house that day its fastening in the evening was overlooked."

"Even if a second person had let himself down from the window," the inspector argued, "the rope would have been here."

Henshaw kept silence, seemingly indifferent to the officials' arguments. "I can only tell you I am far from satisfied with the suicide theory," he said at length. "My brother was not that sort of man. He had nerves of iron; he was in love with life and all it meant to him, and he made it a rule never to let anything worry him. Let the other fellow worry, was his motto. Well, we shall see."

He turned towards the door, and as he did so he caught sight of a cardboard box in which was a collection of various articles, jewellery, a watch and chain, money, a pocket-handkerchief, a letter, and a dance programme.

"The contents of deceased's pockets," the inspector observed, answering Henshaw's glance of curiosity. "We have collected and made a list of them, and they will in due course be handed to you, or to his heir, on the coroner's order."

"Is that a letter? May I see it?"

As the official hesitated, Henshaw had snatched the paper, a folded note, and rapidly ran his eye through its contents. Then he gave a curious laugh, as he turned over the paper as though seeking an address, and laid it back in the box.

"A note from my brother to an anonymous lady," he observed quietly. "Perhaps if we could find out whom it was meant for she would throw some light on the mystery."

8
KELSON'S PERPLEXITY

"What do you think of Mr. Gervase Henshaw?" Kelson said, as, late in the afternoon, he and Gifford walked towards the town together. Henshaw had left Wynford Place half an hour previously, having kept to the end his attitude of resentful incredulity.

"A nailer," Gifford answered shortly.

"Yes," Kelson agreed. "He gives one the idea of a man who will make trouble if he can. As offensive as his brother was, I should say, although in a different line. I did not detect one sign of any consideration for the Morristons in their horribly unpleasant position."

"No," Gifford agreed. "I was very sorry for Morriston. He behaved extremely well, considering the irritatingly antagonistic line the man chose to take up."

"Brainy man, Henshaw; unpleasantly sharp, eh?"

"Yes," Gifford replied. "Added to his legal training he is by way of being an expert in criminology."

"I do hope," Kelson remarked thoughtfully, "he is not going to make himself unpleasant down here. The scandal will be quite enough without that. Horribly rough luck on the Morristons as new-comers here to have an affair like this happening in their house. I can't think what brought the man down here."

"No; he came with a purpose, that's certain."

"A woman in it, no doubt. One can quite sympathize with the brother's incredulity as to the suicide theory, though hardly with his manner of showing it. The dead man was not that sort. The idea is simply staggering."

Gifford made no response, and for a while they walked on in silence. Presently he asked, "How did you get on to-day—I mean with Colonel Tredworth?"

"Oh, everything went off beautifully," Kelson answered, his tone brightening with the change of subject. "The old boy gave me his consent and his blessing. I've scarcely been able as yet to appreciate my luck, with this affair at Wynford Place intervening."

"No," Gifford responded mechanically. "It is calculated to drive everything else out of one's head."

"It is suggested," said Kelson, "that we should be married quite soon. The Tredworths are going abroad next month and don't propose to hurry back. So it means that if the wedding does not take place before they leave it must be postponed till probably the autumn."

"I should think the latter would be the best plan."

Kelson turned quickly to his companion. "To postpone it?" he exclaimed in a rather hurt tone. "Why on earth should we? We have nothing to wait for; I mean money or anything of that sort."

"No; but settlements take a long time to draw up."

"Not if the lawyers are told to hurry up with them."

"Then you will have to find a house, and get furniture. And there is the trousseau," Gifford urged.

"Oh," Kelson returned with a show of impatience, "all these details can be got over in two or three weeks if we set ourselves to do it. I don't believe in waiting once the thing is settled."

"I don't believe in rushing matters," Gifford rejoined. "Least of all matrimony."

Kelson stopped dead. "Why, Hugh," he said in an expostulatory tone, "what is the matter with you? You are most confoundedly unsympathetic. Any one would think you did not want me to marry the girl."

"I certainly don't want you to be in too great a hurry," Gifford returned calmly.

"But why? Why?"

"I feel it is a mistake."

Kelson laughed. "You are not going to suggest we don't know our own minds."

"Hardly. But why not wait till the family returns? Of course it is no business of mine."

"No," Kelson replied with a laugh of annoyance; "and you can't be expected to enter into my feelings on the subject. But I think you might be a little less grudging of your sympathy."

"You quite mistake me, Harry," Gifford replied warmly. "It is only in your own interest that I counsel you not to be in a hurry."

"But why? What, in heaven's name, do you mean?" Kelson demanded, vaguely apprehensive.

"It is a mistake to rush things, that is all," was the unsatisfactory answer.

"If I saw the slightest chance of danger I would not hesitate to take your advice," Kelson said. "But I don't. Nor do you. Since when have you become so cautious?"

Gifford forced a laugh. "It is coming on with age."

Kelson clapped him on the shoulder. "Don't encourage it, my dear Hugh. It will spoil all the enjoyment in your life, and in other people's too, if you force the note. I promise you I won't hurry on the wedding more than is absolutely necessary."

"Very well," Gifford responded, and the subject dropped.

They had finished dinner, at which the absorbing subject of the tragedy at Wynford Place was the main topic of their conversation, when the landlord came in to say that Mr. Gervase Henshaw, who was staying at the hotel, would like to see them if they were disengaged.

Kelson looked across at his friend. "Shall we see him?"

Gifford nodded. "We had better hear what he has to say. We don't want him worrying Morriston."

"Ask Mr. Henshaw up," Kelson said to the landlord, and in a minute he was ushered in.

With a quick, decisive movement Henshaw took the seat to which Kelson invited him.

"I trust you won't think me intrusive, gentlemen," he began in his sharp mode of speaking, "but you will understand I am very much upset and horribly perplexed by the terrible fate which has overtaken my poor brother. I am setting myself to search for a clue, if ever so slight, to the mystery, the double mystery, I may say, and it occurred to me that perhaps a talk with you gentlemen who are, so far, the last known persons who spoke with him, might possibly give me a hint."

"I'm afraid there is very little we can tell you," Gifford replied. "But we are at your service."

"Thank you." It seemed the first civil word of acknowledgment they had heard him utter. "First of all," he proceeded, falling back to his dry, lawyer-like tone, "I have been to see the medical man who was summoned to look at the body, Dr. Page. He tells me that, so far as his cursory examination went, the position of the wound hardly suggests that it was self-inflicted."

"Is he sure of it?" Kelson asked.

"He won't be positive till he has made the autopsy," Henshaw answered. "He merely suggests that it was a very awkward and altogether unlikely place for a man to wound himself. Anyhow that guarded opinion is enough to strengthen my inclination to scout the idea of suicide."

"Then," said Kelson, "we are faced by the difficulty of the locked door."

Henshaw made a gesture of indifference.

"That at first sight presents a problem, I admit," he said, "but not so complete as to look absolutely insoluble. I have, as you may be aware, made a study of criminology, and in my researches, which have included criminality, have come across incidents which to the smartest detective brains were at the outset quite as baffling. Clement's tragic end is a great blow to me, and I am not going quietly to accept the easy, obvious conclusion of suicide. I knew and appreciated my brother better than that. I mean to probe this business to the bottom."

"You will be justified," Kelson murmured.

"I think so—by the result," was the quick rejoinder.

Gifford spoke. "What do you think was the real object in your brother coming down here?"

Henshaw looked at his questioner keenly before he answered. "It is my opinion, my conviction, there was a lady in the case. May I ask what prompted you to ask the question?"

Gifford shrugged. "Some idea of the sort was in my own mind," he replied, with a reserve which could scarcely be satisfying to Henshaw.

"Perhaps," he said keenly, "you have also an idea who the lady was."

Gifford shook his head. "Not at all," he returned promptly.

"Then why should the idea have suggested itself to you," came the cross-examining rejoinder.

"Your brother was not a member of the Hunt, and it seemed to us—curious."

Henshaw took him up quickly. "That he should come to the ball? No doubt. I will be perfectly frank with you, as I expect you to be with me. It is perhaps not quite seemly to discuss my brother's failings at this time, but we want to get at the truth about his death. He had, I fear, rather irregular methods in his treatment of women. One can hardly blame him, poor fellow. His was a fascinating personality, at any rate so far as women were concerned. They ran after him, and one can scarcely blame him if he acquired a derogatory opinion of them. After all, he held them no cheaper than they made themselves in his eyes. That note I looked at which came from his pocket was written by him to make an assignation."

"Was it addressed?" Gifford put the question quickly, almost eagerly.

"No," Henshaw answered. "I wish it had been. In that case we should be near the end of the mystery."

Kelson was staring at the glib speaker with astounded eyes. "Do you suppose a woman killed your brother?" he almost gasped.

"Such things have been known," Henshaw returned with the flicker of an enigmatical smile. "But no, I don't suggest that–yet. At present I have got no farther than the conviction that Clement did not kill himself. I mean to find out for whom that note of his was intended."

"Not an easy task," Gifford remarked, with his eye furtively on Kelson, who had become strangely interested.

"It may or may not be easy," Henshaw returned. "But it is to be done. The woman who, intentionally or otherwise, drew my brother down here has to be found, and I mean to find her."

Kelson was now staring almost stupidly at Gifford.

"Neither of you gentlemen saw my brother dancing?" Henshaw demanded sharply.

"I saw nothing of him at all in the ballroom," Gifford answered, "as I did not arrive till about midnight. Did you see him, Harry?" he asked, as though with the design of rousing Kelson from his rather suspicious attitude.

Kelson seemed to pull himself together by an effort.

"No–yes; I caught a glimpse of him, I think, with a girl in green."

"You know who she was?" Henshaw demanded.

"I've not the vaguest idea," Kelson answered mechanically. "I did not see her face."

Henshaw rose. Perhaps from Kelson's manner he gathered that the men were tired, and had had enough of him. He shook hands, with a word of thanks and an apology. "We may know more after the inquest to-morrow afternoon," he remarked, "although I doubt it. You will let me consult you again, if necessary? Thanks. Goodnight."

As the door closed on Henshaw, Kelson turned quickly to Gifford with a scared face. "Hugh!" he cried hoarsely, in a voice subdued by fear. "The blood stain on my cuff that night. How did it come there? Was it–?"

Gifford forced a smile. "My dear Harry, how absurd! What could that have had to do with it?"

Kelson gave an uncomfortable laugh. "It is a grim coincidence," he said.

9
THE CLOAK OF NIGHT

At the inquest which was held next day nothing was elicited which could offer any solution of the mystery of Clement Henshaw's death. It seemed to be pretty generally accepted to be a case of suicide, although that view was opposed in evidence, not only by Gervase Henshaw on general grounds, but also by the medical witnesses, who had grave doubts whether the mortal wound had been self-inflicted.

"Just possible but decidedly improbable, both from the position of the wound and the direction of the blow," was Dr. Page's opinion.

It was a downward, oblique stab in the throat which had pierced the larynx and penetrated the jugular vein. The deceased would have been unable to cry out and would probably have quickly become insensible from asphyxiation. Unless he was left-handed the stab could scarcely have been self-given.

The police authorities committed themselves to no definite theory at that stage, and at their request the inquiry was adjourned for a month.

Morriston, leaving the hall with Kelson and Gifford, asked them to walk back with him to Wynford Place.

"Let us throw off this depressing business as well as we can," he said. "Of course I have had to break it to my sister and the others; they would have seen it to-day in print. Thank goodness the papers don't look beyond the suicide idea, so they are not making much fuss about it. If they took a more sensational view, as I fear they will now after the medical evidence, it would be a terrible nuisance."

"I hope the ladies were not much upset when you told them," Gifford remarked.

"Well, they already had an idea that something was seriously wrong, and that took the edge off the announcement. Of course they were horribly shocked at the idea of the tragedy so close at hand, though I softened the details as well as I could."

"If the suicide idea is to be abandoned," said Kelson, speaking with an unusually gloomy, preoccupied air, "the police have an uncommonly difficult and delicate task before them."

"Yes, indeed," Morriston responded. "And I should say that abnormally keen person, the brother, will keep them up to collar."

"He means to," Kelson replied rather grimly. "We had him for an hour last night cross-examining us, naturally to no purpose; we could tell him nothing."

"He won't leave a stone unturned," Morriston said. "He proposes to return here after the funeral in town."

"And I should say," observed Kelson, "if the mystery is to be solved he is the man to solve it. What do you think, Hugh?"

Gifford seemed to rouse himself by an effort from an absorbing train of thought. "Oh, yes," he answered. "Except that it is possible to be a little too clever and so overlook the obvious."

"If," said Morriston, obsessed by the subject, "the case is not one of suicide it must be one of murder. Where is Mr. Gervase Henshaw, or anyone else, going to look for the criminal?"

"Not among your guests, let's hope," Kelson said with a touch of uneasiness.

"For one thing," Morriston replied, "they, or a good part of them, were not exactly my guests. I can't tell who may have got a ticket and been present. There was a great crowd. We may have easily rubbed shoulders with the murderer, if murder it was."

"Yes, so we may," said Kelson alertly, though with something of a shudder.

"Not a pleasant idea," continued Morriston. "But I don't see, if a bad character did get in and mix with the company, why he should have done a fellow guest to death, nor how he contrived to leave his victim and get out of the room after he had locked the door."

"If the two men had a row over a girl, or anything else," Kelson said, "there is still that difficulty to be surmounted."

Gifford spoke. "From what one could judge of the dead man's personality and character it is not a far-fetched supposition that he must have had enemies."

"Down here?" Morriston objected incredulously. "Where he was a stranger? Unless some ingenious person, bent on vengeance, tracked him here and then lured him into the tower. Then how did the determined pursuer contrive to leave him and the key inside the locked room?"

At Wynford Place, where they had now arrived, they found several callers. The subject of the tragedy was naturally uppermost in everybody's mind, and the principal topic of conversation. Morriston and his companions were eagerly questioned as to what had come out at the inquest, but, except that the medical evidence was rather sceptical of the suicide theory, were unable to relieve the curiosity.

"I think, my dear Dick," remarked Lord Painswick, who was there, "we can furnish more evidence in this room than you seem to have got hold of at the inquest." And he looked round the company with a knowing smile.

"What do you mean, Painswick?" Morriston asked eagerly. "Has anything more come to light?"

"Only we have had a lady here, Miss Elyot, who says she danced with the poor fellow."

"I only just took a turn with him, for the waltz was nearly over when he asked me," said the girl thus alluded to.

"Did you wear a green dress?" Kelson asked eagerly.

"Yes. Why?"

"Only that it must have been you I saw with him."

"And can you throw any light on the mystery?" Morriston asked.

The girl shook her head. "None at all, I'm afraid."

"Did Mr. Henshaw's manner or state of mind strike you as being peculiar?"

"Not in the least," Miss Elyot answered with decision. "During the short time we were together our talk was quite commonplace, mostly of the changes in the county."

"Did he, Henshaw, know it formerly?" Morriston asked with some surprise.

"Oh, yes," Miss Elyot answered, "he used to stay with some people over at Lamberton; you remember the Peltons, Muriel?" she turned to Miss Tredworth. "Of course you do."

"Oh, yes," Muriel Tredworth answered. "I remember them quite well, although we didn't know much about them."

"Don't you recollect," Miss Elyot continued, "meeting this very Mr. Henshaw at a big garden party they gave. I know you played tennis with him."

"Did I?" Miss Tredworth replied. "What a memory you have, Gladys. You can't expect me to recollect every one of the scores of men I must have played tennis with."

As she spoke she caught Gifford's eye; he was watching her keenly, more closely perhaps than manners or tact warranted. "And do you find the place much changed since your time, Mr. Gifford?" she inquired, as though to relieve the awkwardness.

"Not as much as I could have imagined," he answered, through what seemed a fit of preoccupation.

"Mr. Gifford has not had much opportunity yet of seeing how far it has altered, with this tragic affair to upset everything," Morriston put in.

"No, it has been a most unlucky time for him to revisit Wynford," Miss Morriston added in her cold tone. "I hope Mr. Gifford is not going to hurry away from the neighbourhood in consequence."

"Not if I can prevent it," Kelson replied, with a laugh.

"I hope," Morriston said hospitably, "that whether his stay be short or long Mr. Gifford will consider himself quite at home here. And I need not say, my dear Kelson, that invitation includes you."

Both men thanked him. "We have already done a little trespassing in your park," Kelson observed with a laugh.

"Please don't call it trespassing again," Miss Morriston commanded. "Let me give you another cup of tea, Muriel."

"The old house looks most picturesque by moon-light," observed Lord Painswick. "I was quite fascinated by it the other night."

"There is a full moon now," Gifford said. "We will stroll round and admire when we leave."

"Don't stroll over the edge of the haha as I very nearly did one night," Morriston said laughingly. "When it lies in the shadow of the house it is a regular trap."

"Moonlight has its dangers as well as its beauties," Painswick murmured sententiously.

"The friendly cloak of night is apt to trip one up," Gifford added.

As he spoke the words there came a startling little cry from Miss Tredworth accompanied by the crash and clatter of falling crockery. Gifford's remark had been made with his eyes fixed on his friend's *fiancée*, to whom at that moment Miss Morriston was handing the refilled cup of tea. A hand of each girl was upon the saucer as the words were uttered; by whose fault it was let fall it was impossible to say. But the slight cry of dismay had come from Miss Tredworth.

"Oh, I am so sorry," she exclaimed, colouring with vexation. "How stupid and clumsy of me. Your lovely china."

"It was my fault," Edith Morriston protested, her clear-cut face showing no trace of annoyance. "I thought you had hold of the cup, and I let it go too soon. Ring the bell, will you, Dick."

"Please don't distress yourself, Miss Tredworth," Mr. Morriston entreated her as he crossed to the bell. "I'm sure it was not your fault."

"Was that a quotation, Mr. Gifford?" Miss Morriston asked, clearly with the object of dismissing the unfortunate episode.

"My remark about the cloak of night?" he replied. "Perhaps. I seem to have heard something like it somewhere."

And as he spoke he glanced curiously at Miss Tredworth.

10
AN ALARMING DISCOVERY

Next evening the two friends at the *Golden Lion* were engaged to dine with the Morristons. They had been out with the hounds all day, and, beyond the natural gossip of the country-side, had heard nothing fresh concerning the tragedy. Gervase Henshaw had gone up to town for his brother's funeral, and Host Dipper had no fresh development to report. In answer to a question from Gifford, he said he expected Mr. Henshaw back on the morrow, or at latest the day after.

"It is altogether a most mysterious affair," he observed sagely, being free, now that his late guest's perplexing disappearance was accounted for, even in that tragic fashion, to regard the business and to moralize over it without much personal feeling in the matter. "I fancy Mr. Gervase Henshaw means to work the police up to getting to the bottom of it. For I don't fancy that he is by any means satisfied that his unfortunate brother took his own life. And I must say," he added in a pronouncement evidently the fruit of careful deliberation, "I don't know how it strikes you, gentlemen, but from what I saw of the deceased it is hard to imagine him as making away with himself."

"Yes," Gifford replied. "But before any other conclusion can be fairly arrived at the police will have to account for the locked door."

Evidently Mr. Dipper's lucubrations had not, so far, reached a satisfactory explanation of that puzzle; he could only wag his head and respond generally, "Ah, yes. That will be a hard nut for them to crack, I'm thinking."

The dinner at Wynford Place was made as cheerful as, with the gloom of a tragedy over the house, could be possible.

"We had the police with a couple of detectives here all this morning," Morriston said, "and a great upset it has been. After having made the most minute scrutiny of the room in the tower they had every one of the servants in one by one and put them through a most searching examination. But, I imagine, without result. No one in the house, and I have questioned most of them casually myself, seems to be able to throw the smallest light on the affair."

"Have the police arrived at any theory?" Gifford inquired.

"Apparently they have come to no definite conclusion," Morriston answered. "They seemed to have an idea, though—to account for the problem of the locked door—that thieves might have got into the house with the object of making a haul in the bedrooms while every one's attention was engaged down below, have secreted themselves in the tower, been surprised by Henshaw, and, to save themselves, have taken the only effectual means of silencing him, poor fellow."

"Then how, with the door locked on the inside did they make their escape?" Miss Morriston asked.

"That can so far be only a matter of conjecture," her brother answered, with a shrug. "Of course they might have provided themselves with some sort of ladder, but there are no signs of it. And the height of the window in that top room is decidedly against the theory."

"We hear at the *Lion*" Kelson remarked, "that the brother, Gervase Henshaw, is returning to-morrow or next day."

Morriston did not receive the news with any appearance of satisfaction. "I hope he won't come fussing about here," he said, with a touch of protest. "Making every allowance for the sudden shock under which he was labouring I thought his attitude the other day most objectionable, didn't you?"

"I did most certainly," Gifford answered promptly.

"His manners struck me as deplorable," Kelson agreed.

"Yes," their host continued. "It never seemed to occur to the fellow that some little sympathy was due also to us. But he seemed rather to suggest that the tragedy was our fault. In ordinary circumstances I should have dealt pretty shortly with him. But it was not worthwhile."

"No," Kelson observed, "All the same, you need not allow a continuation of his behaviour."

"I don't intend to," Morriston replied with decision. "I hope the man won't want to come ferreting in the place; that may well be left to the police; but if he does I can't very well refuse him leave. He must be free of the house, or at any rate of the tower."

"Or," put in Kelson, "he'll have a grievance against you, and accuse you of trying to burk the mystery."

"Is he a very objectionable person?" Miss Morriston asked. "We passed one another in the hall as he left the house and I received what seemed a rather unmannerly stare."

Her brother laughed. "My dear Edith, the type of man you would simply loathe. Abnormally, unpleasantly sharp and suspicious; with a cleverness which takes no account of tact or politeness, he questions you as though you were in the witness-box and he a criminal barrister trying to trap you. I don't know whether he behaves more civilly to ladies, but from our experience of the man I should recommend you to keep out of his way."

"I shall," his sister replied.

"I should say no respecter of persons—or anything else," Kelson remarked with a laugh.

"Let us hope he won't take it into his head to worry us," Miss Morriston said with quiet indifference.

"I am sorry to see," Morriston observed later on when the ladies had left them, "that the papers are beginning to take a sensational view of the affair."

"Yes," Kelson responded; "we noticed that. It will be a nuisance for you."

"The trouble has already begun," his host continued somewhat ruefully. "We have had two or three reporters here to-day worrying the servants with all sorts of absurd questions. It is, of course, all to be accounted for by the medical evidence. That has put them on the scent of what they will no doubt call a sensational development. So long as it looked like nothing beyond suicide there was not so much likelihood of public interest in the case."

"The police—" Gifford began.

"The police," Morriston took up the word, "are fairly nonplussed. It seems the farther they get the less obvious does the suicide theory become. Well, we shall see."

"In the meantime I'm afraid you and Miss Morriston are in for a heap of undeserved annoyance," Kelson observed sympathetically.

"Yes," Morriston agreed gloomily; "I am sorry for Edith; she is plucky, and feels it, I expect, far more than she cares to show."

When the men went into the drawing-room Muriel Tredworth made a sign to Kelson; he joined her and, sitting down some distance apart from the rest, they carried on in low tones what seemed to be a serious conversation.

"I want to tell you of something extraordinary which has happened to me, Hugh." Gifford just caught the words as the girl led the way out of earshot. He had noticed that she had been rather preoccupied during dinner, an unusual mood for so lively a girl, and now he could not help watching the pair in the distance, she talking with an earnest, troubled expression, and he listening to her story in grave wonderment, now and again interposing a few words. Once they looked at Gifford, and he was certain they were speaking of him.

With the gloom of a tragedy over the house the little party could not be very festive; avoid it as they set themselves to do, the brooding subject could not be ignored, general conversation flagged, and it soon became time for the visitors to say good-night.

As they walked back to the town together Gifford noticed that his companion was unusually silent, and he tactfully forbore to break in upon his preoccupation. At length Kelson spoke.

"Muriel has just been telling me of an unpleasant and unaccountable thing which happened to her this evening. A discovery of a rather alarming character. I said I would take your advice about it, Hugh, and she agreed."

"Does it concern the affair at Wynford?"

"It may," Kelson answered in a perplexed tone; "and yet I don't well see how it can. Anyhow it is uncommonly mysterious. We won't talk about it here," he added gravely, "but wait till we get in."

"Miss Morriston looked well to-night," Gifford remarked, falling in with his friend's wish to postpone the more engrossing subject.

"Yes," Kelson agreed casually. "She takes this ghastly business quietly enough. But that is her way."

"I have been wondering," Gifford said, "how much she cares for Painswick. He is manifestly quite smitten, but I doubt her being nearly as keen on him."

Kelson laughed. "If you ask me I don't think she cares a bit for him. And one can scarcely be surprised. He is not a bad fellow, but rather a prig, and Edith Morriston is not exactly the sort of girl to suffer that type of man gladly. But her brother is all for the match; from Painswick's point of view she is just the wife for him, money and a statuesque style of beauty; altogether I shall be surprised if it does not come off."

"They are not engaged, then?"

"I think not. They say he proposes regularly once a week. But she holds him off."

Arrived at the *Golden Lion* they went straight up to Kelson's room, where with more curiosity than he quite cared to show, Gifford settled himself to hear what the other had to tell him.

"I dare say you noticed how worried Muriel looked all dinner-time," Kelson began. "I thought that what had happened in the house had got on her nerves; but it was something worse than that; I mean touching her more nearly."

"Tell me," Gifford said quietly.

"You know," Kelson proceeded, "they are going to this dance at Hasborough to-morrow. Well, it appears that when her maid was overhauling her ball-dress, the same she wore here the other night, she found blood stains on it."

"That," Gifford remarked coolly, "may satisfactorily account for the marks on your cuff."

Kelson stared in surprise at the other's coolness.

"I dare say it does," he exclaimed with a touch of impatience. "I had hardly connected the two. But what do you think of this? How in the name of all that's mysterious can it be accounted for?"

"Hardly by the idea that Miss Tredworth had anything to do with the late tragedy," was the quiet answer.

"Good heavens, man, I should hope not," Kelson cried vehemently. "That is too monstrously absurd."

"What is Miss Tredworth's idea?"

"She has none. She is completely mystified. And inclined to be horribly frightened."

"Naturally," Gifford commented in the same even tone.

His manner seemed to irritate Kelson. "I wish, my dear Hugh, I could take it half as coolly as you do," he exclaimed resentfully.

"I don't know what you want me to do or say, Harry," Gifford expostulated. "The whole affair is so utterly mysterious that I can't pretend even to hazard an explanation."

"In the meantime Muriel and I are in the most appalling position. Why, man, she may at any moment be arrested on suspicion if this discovery leaks out, as it is sure to do."

"You can't try to hush it up; that would be a fatal mistake," Gifford said thoughtfully, "and would immediately arouse suspicion."

"Naturally I am not going to be such a fool as to advise that," Kelson returned. "The discovery will be the subject of the servants' talk till it gets all over the place and into the papers. No, what I have determined to do, unless you see any good reason for the contrary, is to go first thing in the morning to the police and tell them. What do you say?" he added sharply, as Gifford was silent.

"I should not do anything in a hurry," Gifford answered.

"But surely," Kelson remonstrated, "the sooner we take the line of putting ourselves in the right the better."

Again Gifford paused before replying.

"Can Miss Tredworth give no explanation, has she no idea as to how the stains came on her dress?"

"None whatever," was the emphatic answer.

"You are absolutely sure of that?"

Kelson jumped up from his chair. "Hugh, what are you driving at?" he cried, his eyes full of vague suspicion. "I–I don't understand the cool way you are taking this. There is something behind it. Tell me. I will know; I have a right."

Evidently the man was almost beside himself with the fear of something he could not comprehend. Gifford rose and laid a hand sympathetically on his shoulder. "I am sorry to seem so brutal, Harry," he said gently, "but this discovery does not surprise me."

Kelson recoiled as from a blow, staring at his friend with a horror-struck face. "Why, good heavens, what do you mean?" he gasped.

"Only," Gifford answered calmly, "that when you introduced me to Miss Tredworth at the dance I noticed the stains on the white flowers she wore."

"You did?" Kelson was staring stupidly at Gifford. "And you knew they were blood-stains?"

"I could not tell that," was the answer. "But now it is pretty certain they were."

For some seconds neither man spoke. Then with an effort Kelson seemed to nerve himself to put another question.

"Hugh," he said, his eyes pitiful with fear, "you—you don't think Muriel Tredworth had anything to do with Henshaw's death?"

Gifford turned away, and leaned on the mantelpiece.

"I don't know what to think," he said gloomily.

11
GIFFORD'S COMMISSION

Next morning directly after breakfast Kelson started for Wynford Place. As the result of deliberating fully upon the anxious problem before them, he and Gifford had come to the conclusion that it might be a grave mistake to try to keep secret the maid's discovery. It would doubtless by this time have become a subject of gossip and speculation in the household and consequently would very soon become public. Accordingly it was arranged that Kelson should arrive first and have a private interview with Muriel Tredworth with a view to ascertaining finally and for certain whether she could in any way account for the stain on her dress. Gifford was to follow half an hour later, when they would have a conference with the Morristons and afterwards, with their approval, go into the town and see the chief constable on the subject. If Gifford was doubtful as to the expediency of the plan, and it was with a considerable amount of hesitation that he brought himself to agree to it, he seemed to have no good reason to urge against it. And, after all, it appeared, in the circumstances, the only politic course to follow. Secrecy was practically now out of the question, and any attempt in that direction would inevitably fail and would in all probability produce results unpleasant to contemplate.

When Gifford arrived at Wynford Place he found Kelson pacing the drive and impatiently expecting him.

"Come along," he exclaimed, "the Morristons are waiting for us."

"Miss Tredworth–?"

"Is utterly unable to account for the state of her dress," Kelson declared promptly. "She is positive that if she noticed the man she never spoke a word to him, nor danced with him. She says that if she ever met him before, as according to that girl the other day was the case, she had quite forgotten the circumstance. So the sooner we communicate this discovery to the police the better. As it is, they say the servants are talking of it; so the present position is quite intolerable."

In the library they found Morriston and his sister with the Tredworths. The situation was discussed and there seemed no doubt in the mind of any one of the party that the only thing to be done was to inform the police at once.

"The whole affair is so mysterious," Morriston said, "that all sorts of absurd rumours will be afloat if we don't take a strong, straightforward line at once. Don't you agree, Edith?"

"Certainly I do," Miss Morriston answered with decision. "I don't suppose," she added with a smile, "that anyone would be mad enough to suggest, my dear Muriel, that you were in any way implicated in the affair; but the world is full of stupid and ill-natured people and one can't be too careful to put oneself in the right. Don't you agree, Captain Kelson?"

"Most decidedly," Kelson replied, with a troubled face. Charlie Tredworth was also quite emphatically of opinion that his sister should make no secret of what had been found.

"The inspector, who is here," Morriston said, "tells me that Major Freeman, our chief constable, intends to come here this morning. I'll say we want to see him directly he arrives."

It was not long before the chief constable was shown into the library. Morriston lost no time in telling him of the mysterious circumstance which had come to light. Major Freeman, a keen soldierly man, with the stern expression and uncompromising manner naturally acquired by those whose business is to deal with crime, received the information with grave perplexity. He turned a searching look upon Muriel Tredworth.

"I understand you are quite unable to account for the stains on your dress, Miss Tredworth?" he asked in a tone of courteous insistence.

"Quite," she answered. "I did not speak to Mr. Henshaw or even notice him in the ball-room."

"You had—pardon these questions; I am putting this in your own interest—you had at no time any acquaintance with Mr. Clement Henshaw?"

"I can hardly say that I had," the girl replied; "although a friend has told me that I played tennis with him at a garden-party some years ago."

"A circumstance which you do not recollect?" The question was put politely, even sympathetically, yet with a certain uncomfortable directness.

"No," Muriel answered. "Even when I was reminded of it, my recollection was of the vaguest description. So far as that goes I could neither admit nor deny it with any certainty."

"And naturally you never, to your knowledge, saw or communicated with the deceased man since?"

Muriel flushed. "No; absolutely no," she returned with a touch of resentment at the suggestion.

Major Freeman forbore to distress the girl by any further questioning. "Thank you," he said simply. "I am sorry to have even appeared to suggest such a thing, but you and your friends will appreciate that it was my duty to ask these questions. This looks at the moment," he continued, addressing himself now to the party in general, "like proving a very mysterious, and I will add, peculiarly delicate affair. The medical evidence is inclined to scout the idea of suicide, and my men who have the case in hand are coming round to the conclusion that the theory is untenable."

"The locked door—" Morriston suggested.

"The locked door," said Major Freeman, "presents a difficulty, but still one not absolutely incapable of solution. We know," he added, with a faint smile, "from the way the door was eventually opened, that a key can be turned from the other side, given the right instrument to effect it."

"Which only a burglar or a locksmith would be likely to have," Kelson suggested.

Major Freeman nodded. "Quite so. I am not for a moment suggesting that as an explanation of the mystery. It goes naturally much deeper than that. Mr. Gervase Henshaw is to look into his brother's affairs and papers while in town, and I am hoping that on his return here he may be able to give some information which will afford a clue on which we can work. In the meantime my men are not relaxing their efforts in this rather baffling case."

"In which," Morriston suggested, "this new piece of evidence does not afford any useful clue."

Major Freeman smiled, a little awkwardly, it seemed. "If anything, it would appear to complicate the problem still further," he replied guardedly. "Still, I am very glad to have it, and thank you for informing me so promptly. Miss Tredworth may rest assured that should we find it necessary to go still farther into this piece of evidence, it will be done with as little annoyance as possible."

Some of the chief constable's habitual sternness of manner seemed to have returned to him as he now rose to take leave. "I will just confer with my men who are on the premises before I leave," he said to Morriston in a quiet authoritative tone. "They may have something to report." With that he bowed to the company and quitted the room, leaving behind him a rather uncomfortable feeling which everyone seemed to make an effort to throw off.

But there was clearly nothing to be done except to let the police researches take their course and to wait for developments. The party at Wynford was going over to the dance at Stowgrave that evening and it was arranged that they would call for Kelson and Gifford and all go on together.

Accordingly at the appointed time the carriage stopped at the *Golden Lion*; Kelson joining Miss Tredworth and her brother, while Gifford drove with Morriston.

In answer to his companion's inquiry Morriston said that he had heard of nothing fresh in the Henshaw case.

"I saw Major Freeman for a moment as he was leaving," he said, "and gathered that the police were still at a loss for any satisfactory explanation as to how the crime was committed."

"He made no suggestion as to the stains on Miss Tredworth's dress?" Gifford asked.

"No. Although I fancy he is a good deal exercised by that piece of evidence. Mentioned, as delicately as possible, that it might be necessary to have the stains analyzed, but did not wish the girl to be alarmed or worried about it. I can't understand," Morriston added in a puzzled tone, "how on earth she could possibly have had anything to do with it."

"No," Gifford assented thoughtfully; "it is inconceivable, unless by the supposition that she may by some means have come in contact with someone who was concerned in the crime."

"You mean if a man had a stain on his coat and danced with her—"

"Something of the sort. If there were blood on his lapel or sleeve."

"H'm! It would be easy to ascertain for certain whom she danced with," Morriston said reflectively. "But that again is almost unthinkable."

"And," Gifford added, "it seems to go no way towards elucidating the problem of how Henshaw came to his death. As a matter of fact I should say Miss Tredworth danced and sat out nearly the whole of the evening with Kelson. You know he proposed at the dance?"

"Yes, I understood that. Poor Kelson; I am sorry for him, and for them both. It is an ominous beginning of their betrothal."

"It is horrible," Gifford observed sympathetically. "Although one tries to think there is really nothing in it for them to be concerned about."

The dance was an enjoyable affair, and, at any rate for the time, dispersed the depression which had hung over the party from Wynford. Gifford had engaged Miss Morriston for two waltzes, and after a turn or two in the second his partner said she felt tired and suggested they should sit out the rest of it. Accordingly they strolled off to an adjoining room and made themselves comfortable in a retired corner, Gifford, nothing loath to have a quiet chat with the handsome girl whose self-possessed manner with its suggestion of underlying strength of feeling was beginning to fascinate and intrigue his imagination.

"It is rather pleasant," she said a little wearily, "to get away from the atmosphere of mystery and police investigation we have been living in at home."

"Which I hope and believe will very soon be over," Gifford responded cheeringly.

Miss Morriston glanced at him curiously. "You believe that?" she returned almost sharply. "How can you think so? It seems to me that with little apparent likelihood of clearing up the mystery, the affair may drag on for weeks."

Gifford answered with a reassuring smile. "Hardly that. If the police can make nothing of it, and they seem to be quite nonplussed, they will have to give up their investigations and fall back on their first theory of suicide."

Leaning back and watching his companion's face in profile as she sat forward, he could see that his suggestion was by no means convincing.

"I wish I could take your view, Mr. Gifford," she returned, with the suggestion of a bitter smile. "I dare say if the authorities were left to themselves they might give up. But you forget a very potent factor in the tiresome business, the brother, Mr. Gervase Henshaw; he will keep them up to the work of investigation, will he not?"

"Up to a certain point, and one can scarcely blame him. But even then, the police are not likely to continue working on his theories when they lead to no result."

"No?" Miss Morriston replied in an unconvinced tone. "But he is–" she turned to him. "Tell me your candid opinion of this Mr. Gervase Henshaw. Is he very–"

"Objectionable?" Gifford supplied as she hesitated. "Unpleasantly sharp and energetic, I should say. Although it is, perhaps, hardly fair to judge a man labouring under the stress of a brother's tragic death."

"He is determined to get to the explanation of the mystery?" The tinge of excitement she had exhibited in her former question had now passed away: she now spoke in her habitual cold, even tone.

"He says so. Naturally he will do all he can to that end. Of course it would be a satisfaction to know for certain how the tragedy came about: not that it matters much otherwise. But unfortunately he rather poses as an expert in criminology, and that will make for pertinacity."

For a moment Miss Morriston kept silent. "It is very unfortunate," she murmured at length. "It will worry poor old Dick horribly. I think he is already beginning to wish he had never seen Wynford."

Gifford leaned forward. "Oh, but, my dear Miss Morriston," he said earnestly, "you and your brother must really not take the matter so seriously. It is all very unpleasant, one must admit, but, after all, except that it happened in your house, I don't see that it affects you."

"You think not," Miss Morriston responded mechanically.

"Indeed I think so." As he spoke Gifford could not help a slight feeling of wonder that this girl, from whom he would have expected an attitude rather of indifference, should allow herself to be so greatly worried by the affair.

For that she was far more troubled than she allowed to appear he was certain. It is her pride, he told himself. A high-bred girl like this would naturally hate the very idea of a sensational scandal under her roof, and all its unpleasant, rather sordid accompaniments. "I wish," he added with a touch of fervour, "that I could persuade you to dismiss any fear of annoyance from your mind."

"I wish you could," she responded dully, with an attempt at a smile. Suddenly she turned to him with more animation in her manner than she had hitherto shown. "Mr. Gifford, you–I–" she hesitated as though at a loss how to put what she wished to say; "I have no right to ask you, who are a comparative stranger, to help us in this–this worry, but if you cared to be of assistance I am sure you could."

"Of course, of course I will," he answered with eager gladness. "Only let me know what you wish and you may command the very utmost I can do. And please don't think of me as a stranger."

Edith Morriston smiled, and to Gifford it was the most fascinating smile he had ever seen. "Only let me know how I can serve you," he said, his pulses tingling.

"I am thinking of my brother," she replied, in a tone so friendly that it neutralized the rather damping effect of the words. "He is worrying over this business more than one who does not know him well would think. I had an idea, Mr. Gifford, that you might help us by, in a way, standing between us, so far as might be possible, and this Mr. Gervase Henshaw. He stays at your hotel, does he not?"

"Yes; he is expected there to-morrow morning, if not to-night."

"You may perhaps," the girl proceeded, "be able–I don't know how, and I have no right to ask it–"

"Please, Miss Morriston!" Gifford pleaded.

"To minimize any annoyance we are likely to suffer through his–his uncomfortable zeal," she resumed hesitatingly. "If not that, you may, if he is friendly with you, have an opportunity of getting to hear something of his plans and ideas, and warning me if he is likely to worry us at Wynford. We don't want the tragedy kept alive indefinitely; it would be intolerable. I am sure you understand how I feel. That is all."

"You may rely on me to the utmost," Gifford assured her fervently, in answer to the question in her eyes.

"Thank you," she said, as she rose. "I felt sure I might ask you this favour and trust you."

She made a slight movement of putting out her hand. The gesture was coldly made; it might, indeed, have been checked, and gone for nothing. But Gifford, keenly on the alert for a sign of regard, was quick to take the hand and press it impulsively.

"You may trust me, Miss Morriston," he murmured.

"Thank you," she responded simply, but, he was glad to notice, with a touch of relief.

She lightly took his arm and they went back to the ball-room.

12
HAD HENSHAW A CLUE?

Next day Gervase Henshaw made his expected reappearance in Branchester. He left his luggage at the *Golden Lion* and then went off to the police-station where he had a long interview with the chief constable. Mindful of his promise to Edith Morriston, Hugh Gifford kept about the town with the object of coming across Henshaw and getting to know, if possible, something of his intentions. The attraction he had, even from their first introduction, felt towards Miss Morriston had become quickly intensified by their strangely confidential talk on the previous evening. So far she was to him something of a puzzle, but a puzzle of the most fascinating kind. It was, perhaps, strangely unaccountable that she should have chosen to invoke his help who was little more than a casual acquaintance; still, he argued as he reviewed the situation, she had probably been drawn to him as the one man on the spot who was likely to be of use to them. Her brother, a good, sensible fellow of some character, was nevertheless an ordinary country gentleman, given up to sport of all kinds and naturally quite unversed in the subtleties of life and character which can be studied only by those who live in the more intellectual atmosphere of cities. The same judgment would apply to his friend Kelson, a chivalrous sportsman, who would unselfishly do anything in his power to be of help, but whose ability and penetration by no means matched his willingness. And probably these men were types of the bulk of the Morristons' friends and acquaintances, at any rate of those who were immediately available. Consequently, Gifford concluded, it had been to himself she had turned in this trouble, influenced no doubt by the idea that a

Londoner with legal training and experience of the world in its many aspects would be the best man she could enlist to help her. That her confidence had been drawn by any particular personal liking he never for one moment admitted; that unfortunately was so far all on one side, whatever hopes the future might hold out to him. Anyhow he blessed his luck that an accident had so quickly broken the ice and established a state of confidential relationship between them. As to there being an adequate reason for alarm Gifford was not inclined to question, since he quite realized that this man Henshaw might easily constitute himself a grave annoyance to the Morristons. A clever girl like Edith Morriston, more sensitive than to a casual observer would appear, had naturally recognized this danger and was anxious to have the man, with his, perhaps, none too scrupulous methods, held in check; and to this service Gifford was only too happy to devote himself, glad beyond measure that the opportunity had been given him by the girl who had filled his thoughts.

It was not until evening that he came across Henshaw, it being to his mind essential not to appear anxious or to seek out the criminologist with the obvious view of getting information as to his plans.

"So you are back again, Mr. Henshaw," he said with a careless nod of greeting as they encountered in the hall of the hotel. "I hear the police have not yet arrived at any satisfactory conclusion."

Henshaw drew back his lips in a slight smile. To Gifford the expression was an ugly one, and he wondered what it portended.

"There is a likelihood of our not being at a loss much longer," Henshaw replied, speaking through his teeth with a certain grim satisfaction.

"What, you have made a discovery?" Gifford exclaimed.

Henshaw's face hardened. "I am not yet at liberty to say what I have found," he returned in an uncompromising tone. "But I think you may take it from me as absolutely certain that my brother did not take his own life."

With pursed lips Gifford nodded acceptance of the statement. "That makes the affair look serious, not to say sensational," he responded. "I suppose one must not ask you whether you have a clue to the perpetrator."

"No, I can hardly say that yet," Henshaw answered with a rather cunning look. "You, as one of our profession, Mr. Gifford, will understand that and the unwisdom of premature statements."

"Certainly I do," Gifford agreed promptly. "And am quite content to restrain my curiosity till I get information from the papers."

Henshaw laughed intriguingly. "There are certain things that don't find their way into the Press," he said meaningly. "The real story in this case may turn out to be one of them."

Eager as he was, Gifford resolved to show no further curiosity. "You know best," he rejoined almost casually. "But I hope for the Morristons' sake the mystery will be soon satisfactorily cleared up."

There was a peculiar glitter in Henshaw's eyes as he replied, "No doubt they are anxious."

"Naturally. They are getting rather worried by all this police fuss."

"Naturally." Henshaw repeated Gifford's word with a curious emphasis. "It is unfortunate for them," he added. "But all the same it is imperative that the manner of my brother's death should be thoroughly investigated."

He nodded, and as unwilling to discuss the matter further, opened a newspaper and turned away.

About noon next day Gifford went with Kelson to Wynford Place. They had seen nothing more of Henshaw who, it seemed, was rather inclined to hold away from them, possibly with a view to avoiding an opportunity of discussing the affair, or because he was occupied in following up some clue he had, or thought he had, got hold of. This was naturally a disappointment to Gifford, who was anxious, on Miss Morriston's behalf, to keep himself posted as to Henshaw's intentions.

"Of course," said Kelson, "the fellow will have heard of the stains found on Muriel's dress, and will set himself to make the most of that discovery. I only hope he won't take to worrying her. She is quite enough upset about it without that."

"Doubtless that is why he is keeping away from us," Gifford observed. "He probably has heard of your engagement."

"And has the decency to see that he cannot very well discuss the matter with us," Kelson added.

On their arrival at Wynford Place Morriston told them that Gervase Henshaw was there with a detective in the room of the tragedy. "There is a decided improvement in his manner to-day," he said with a laugh. "He has been quite considerate and apologetic; so much so that I think I shall have to ask him to stay to luncheon; it seems rather churlish in the circumstances not to do so when the man is actually in the house on what should be to him a very sad business. But you fellows must stay too, to take off some of the strain."

They accepted; Gifford not sorry, for more reasons than one, to stay.

He presently took an opportunity of joining Edith Morriston in the garden.

"I have been keeping a look-out for Mr. Henshaw," he said, as they strolled off down a secluded walk, "but so far have had a chance of speaking to him only once, when I ran across him in the hotel."

"Yes?" she responded, with a scarcely concealed curiosity to hear what had passed.

"He has evidently got hold of some clue, or at least thinks he has," Gifford proceeded. "But what it is he did not tell me. In fact he rather declined to discuss the affair. I fancy he had had a long consultation with the police authorities."

"And he would tell you nothing?"

"Nothing. I rather expected he might have come, as before, to discuss the case with us, but he has made a point of keeping away. I hear, however, from your brother that he seems far less objectionable this time."

Somewhat to Gifford's surprise, she gave a rather grudging assent. "Yes, I suppose he is. I happened to see him on his arrival, and he certainly was polite enough, but it is possible to be even objectionably polite."

Gifford glanced at her curiously, wondering what had taken place to call forth the remark. "I know that," he said. "I do hope the man has not annoyed you. From what your brother told us—"

"Oh, no," she interrupted, "I can't say he has annoyed me—from his point of view." She laughed. "The man tried to be particularly agreeable, I think."

"And succeeded in being the reverse," Gifford added. "I can quite understand. Still, it might be worse."

"Oh, yes," she agreed in a tone which did nothing to abate his curiosity.

The luncheon bell rang out and they turned.

"I haven't thanked you for looking after our interests, Mr. Gifford," the girl said.

"I have unfortunately been able to do nothing," he replied deprecatingly.

"But you have tried," she rejoined graciously, "and it is not your fault if you have not succeeded. It is a comfort to think that we have a friend at hand ready to help us if need be, and I am most grateful."

The unusual feeling in her tone thrilled him.

"I should love to do something worthy of your gratitude," he responded, in a subdued tone.

"You take a lower view of your service than I do," she rejoined as they reached the house, and no more could be said.

At luncheon the improvement which their host had mentioned in Henshaw's attitude was strikingly apparent. His dogmatic self-assertiveness which had before been found so irritating was laid aside; his manner was subdued, his tone was sympathetic as he apologized for all the annoyance to which his host and hostess were being put. Gifford, watching him alertly, wondered at the change, and more particularly at its cause, which set him speculating. What did it portend? It seemed as though the complete alteration in the man's attitude and manner might indicate that he had got the solution of the mystery, and no longer had that problem to worry him. Certainly there was little to find fault with in him to-day.

One thing, however, Gifford did not like, and that was Henshaw's rather obvious admiration for Edith Morriston. When they took their places at table, she had motioned to Gifford to sit beside her, and from that position it gradually forced itself upon his notice that Henshaw scarcely took his eyes off his hostess, addressing most of his conversation, and he was a fluent talker, to her. It was, of course, scarcely to be wondered at that this handsome, capable girl should call forth any man's admiration. Gifford himself was indeed beginning to fall desperately in love with her, but this naturally made Henshaw's rather obvious prepossession none the less disagreeable to him. This, then, he reflected, was the explanation of what Miss Morriston had hinted at, what she had described as his objectionable excess of politeness at their meeting that morning. Happily, however, Gifford felt secure in his position as her accredited ally and in her expressed dislike to the man whom it seemed she had unwittingly fascinated. It was indeed unthinkable that this splendid, high-bred girl could ever be responsive to the advances of this unpleasantly sharp, rather underbred man, and he was a little surprised that she could respond to his remarks quite so genially, with more graciousness indeed than even her position as hostess called forth.

He could not quite reconcile it with the way she had spoken of him previously; but then he told himself that he was making too much of the business, and saw what was mere politeness through the magnifying glasses of jealousy. And so, secure in his position, he proceeded to view Henshaw's attempts to ingratiate himself with an amused equanimity.

13
WHAT GIFFORD SAW IN THE WOOD

During the next day or two Gifford saw next to nothing of Gervase Henshaw. They had parted amicably enough after luncheon at Wynford Place; indeed, the change in Henshaw's demeanour had been something of a puzzle to the two friends, although Kelson did not seem much exercised by it. "The fellow has evidently come to the conclusion that in dealing with people like the Morristons an offensive brow-beating manner does not pay," he remarked casually. Gifford, however, had an idea that the reason for the change lay somewhat deeper than that. He wondered whether in the absence of any other apparent cause, Edith Morriston's attractiveness had had anything to do with it. It was not a pleasant idea; still, if it saved her annoyance that would be something gained, he thought; and that it should have any farther result was out of the question.

He had not had that day an opportunity of any private talk with Miss Morriston, for she had driven out after luncheon to pay a call. But a certain suggestion of warmth in her leave-taking had assured him that she still looked for his help and that the conditions were not changed.

What he had undertaken so eagerly was now, however, not easy of accomplishment. For reasons at which Gifford could only guess, Henshaw seemed to be playing an elusive game; he kept out of sight, or, at any rate, avoided all intercourse with the two friends, and on the rare occasions when they met he was to Gifford tantalizingly uncommunicative.

That something was evidently behind his reticence made it all the more unsatisfactory, since the result was that Gifford had no object in going to Wynford Place, for he had nothing to tell. Indeed he learnt more from the Morristons than from Henshaw. The police had concluded their investigations on the premises, much to the relief of the household, who were now left in peace.

"They don't seem to have come to any definite conclusion as to how the tragedy happened," Morriston said. "They have an idea, as I gather from Major Freeman, where to look for the murderer, if murder it was; which I am rather inclined to doubt."

"Is Henshaw likely to give up the search?" Gifford asked.

Morriston looked puzzled. "I can't make out," he answered in a slightly perplexed tone. "Even Freeman does not seem to know what his idea is. He is still about here."

"Yes," Gifford replied. "I caught a glimpse of him this morning."

"Curious," Morriston remarked. "I came across the fellow yesterday afternoon in the big plantation here. He was mooning about and didn't seem best pleased to see me, but he was quite duly apologetic, said he was puzzling over the tragedy and hoped I didn't mind his trespassing on my property. Of course I told him he was free to come and go as he liked, but it did strike me as peculiar that he should be thinking out the case in that plantation which has no possible connection with the scene of the crime."

"Yes, it was curious," Gifford agreed reflectively. "Did he tell you what he was doing about the business?"

Morriston shook his head. "No; he wasn't communicative; didn't seem to have much to go upon. Of course one can't tell what the fellow has at the back of his mind, but I was rather surprised that a Londoner of his energy and smartness should spend his time loafing about down here with what seems a poor chance of any result; and I nearly told him so."

"Perhaps it is as well you didn't," Gifford replied. "He is suspicious enough to imagine you might have a motive in wanting to get rid of him."

Morriston laughed. "I have. He is not exactly the man one wants to have prowling about the place; but it would not be polite to hint as much."

The episode, trivial as it seemed to Morriston, gave Gifford food for disagreeable reflection. Why, indeed, should Henshaw be hanging about in the grounds of Wynford, and give so unconvincing a reason? What troubled Gifford most was that the man's reticent attitude precluded all hope of his learning anything of his plans which could usefully be imparted to Miss Morriston. Evidently there was nothing to be got out of him; the rather open confidence he had displayed on his first appearance at Branchester had quite disappeared, and if Gifford was to find out anything worth reporting it would assuredly not be due to any communication from the man himself.

He had accordingly to be content with the resolve to keep a wary eye on Henshaw's movements.

He was now pretty free to do this. The Tredworths had ended their visit at Wynford and had returned home, and naturally Kelson spent much of his time over there, leaving Gifford to his own devices. It had, in view of Gifford's commission from Miss Morriston, been arranged that he should share Kelson's rooms at the *Golden Lion*, no longer as a guest, so that both men were now independent of each other. The date of Kelson's wedding seemed now likely to be put off for some months, as his friend had suggested. The unpleasant episode of the stains on Muriel Tredworth's dress had, although there was no indication of attaching serious importance to them, nevertheless cast an uncomfortable shadow over the happiness of her betrothal, and without giving any specific reason she had declared for a postponement of

the wedding, for which there was, after all, a quite
natural reason.

"Perhaps it is just as well," Kelson remarked to his
friend. "Although it is absolutely unthinkable that Muriel
could have had anything to do with the affair, yet one can
quite appreciate her wish to wait till perhaps something
crops up to give us the explanation beyond all question. It
is rather a blow to me, and I hope if the mysterious Mr.
Gervase Henshaw is really on the track of the crime he
will produce his solution without much more delay. For a
girl like Muriel to have even the faintest suspicion
hanging over her is simply hateful."

Meanwhile the mysterious Mr. Henshaw seemed in no
hurry to make known his theory, if he had one. Yet he
still remained in Branchester, writing all the morning
and going out in the afternoon, usually with a handful of
letters for post. He always nodded affably to Gifford when
they met, but beyond a casual remark on the weather or
the events of the day, showed no disposition to chat.

But now while Gifford was in this unsatisfactory state
of mind, persevering yet baffled in what he had
undertaken to do, a very singular thing came to pass. He
strolled out one afternoon, aimlessly, wondering whether
the negative result of his efforts justified his remaining in
the place, and yet loath to leave it, held there as he was
by the attraction of Edith Morriston. He felt he could be
making but little way in her favour seeing how he was
failing in what he had undertaken to do for her, and as he
walked he discussed with himself whether it would not be
possible to hit on some more active plan of becoming
acquainted with Henshaw's knowledge and intentions. It
was obviously a delicate business, and after all, he
thought, now that the man's undesirable presence had
practically ceased to be an annoyance to the Morristons
there scarcely seemed any need to bother about him. On
the other hand, however, there was a certain strong
curiosity on his own part to know Henshaw's design and
what kept him in the town.

Gifford's walk took him over well remembered ground. He was strolling along a path which led through the Wynford property, over a rustic bridge across a stream he had often fished when a boy, and so on into a wood which formed one of the home coverts. Making his way through this familiar haunt of by-gone days he came to one of the long rides which bisected the wood for some quarter of a mile. He turned into this and was just looking out for a comfortable trunk where he might sit and smoke, when he caught sight of two figures in the distance ahead walking slowly just on the fringe of the ride. A man and a woman; their backs were towards him, but his blood gave a leap at the sight as their identity flashed upon him. It was, in its unexpectedness, an almost appalling sight to him, as he realised that the two were none other than Henshaw and Edith Morriston.

14
GIFFORD'S PERPLEXITY

Next moment Gifford had instinctively sprung back into the covert of the trees, almost dazed by what he had seen. Henshaw and Edith Morriston! Could it be possible? His eyes must have deceived him. About the girl there could be no doubt. Her tall, graceful figure was unmistakable. But the man. Surely he had been mistaken there; it must have been her brother, or perhaps a friend who had been lunching with them. Had Gifford, his mind obsessed by Henshaw, jumped to a false conclusion? He stooped, and creeping warily beyond the fringe of trees looked after the pair.

They were now some thirty yards away. There could be no doubt that the lady was Edith Morriston; and the man? Incredible as it might seem, he was surely Gervase Henshaw. Gifford had seen him some two hours earlier, and now recognized his grey suit and dark felt hat. He stayed, crouched down, looking after the amazing pair, seeking a sign that the man was not Henshaw. After all, it was, he told himself, more likely that he had made a mistake than that Miss Morriston could be strolling in confidential talk (for such seemed the case) with that fellow. It was too astounding for belief.

They had stopped now, at the end of the ride; the man talking earnestly, it seemed; Miss Morriston standing with head bent down and scoring the grass with her walking-stick as though in doubt or consideration. Would they turn and put the man's identity beyond uncertainty?

Gifford had not long to wait. Miss Morriston seemed to draw off and began to walk back down the ride; her companion turned and promptly put himself by her side.

There was no doubt now as to who he was. Gervase Henshaw.

As one glance, now that the face was revealed, proved that, Gifford drew back quickly and hurried deeper into the thick wood fearful lest his footsteps should be heard. When he had gone a safe distance an intense curiosity made him halt and turn. From his place of hiding he could just see the light of the ride along which the couple would pass. He hated the idea of spying upon Edith Morriston; after all, if she chose to walk and talk with this man it was no business of his; but a supreme distrust of Henshaw, unreasonable enough, perhaps, but none the less keen, made him suspicious that the man might be playing some cowardly game, might have drawn the girl to him by unfair means. Otherwise it was surely inconceivable that she should have consented— condescended indeed–to meet him in that clandestine manner.

As Gifford stayed, hesitating between a breach of good form and a legitimate desire to learn whether the girl was being subjected to unfair treatment, the sound of Henshaw's rather penetrating voice came into earshot, and a few seconds later they passed across the line of Gifford's sight.

He could catch but a glimpse of them through the intervening trees as they went by slowly, but it was enough to tell him that Henshaw was talking earnestly, arguing, it seemed, and on Edith Morriston's clear-cut face was a look of trouble which was not good to see. It made Gifford flush with anger to think that this lovely high-bred girl was being worried, probably being made love to, by a man of that objectionable type; for that she could be in that situation without coercion was not to be believed. The reason for Henshaw's prolonged and rather puzzling stay in the place was now accounted for. Moreover, to Gifford's bitter reflection the whole business seemed clear enough. Henshaw had been caught and fascinated by Edith Morriston's beauty, and being, as was obvious, a man of energy and determination, was now in some subtle way making use of the tragedy as a means of forcing his unwelcome attentions on her. How otherwise could this astounding familiarity be arrived at? Sick with disgust and indignation, Gifford turned away and retraced his steps through the wood, dismissing, as likely to lead to a false position, his first impulse to appear on the scene and stop, at any rate for that day, Henshaw's designs. He felt that to act precipitately might do less good than harm. He was, after all, on private ground there, and had no right to intrude upon what in all likelihood Miss Morriston wished to be a secluded interview. What course he would take in the future was another matter, and one which demanded instant and serious consideration. The right line to adopt was indeed a perplexing problem.

Gifford recalled Morriston's story of having met Henshaw hanging about more or less mysteriously in the plantation, and the annoyance he had expressed at the encounter. The reason was plain enough now. Of course the man was waiting either to waylay Edith Morriston or to meet her by appointment. It was not a pleasant reflection; since the fact showed that these clandestine meetings had probably been going on for some days past. That Henshaw's object was more or less disreputable could not be doubted, and to Gifford the amazing and troubling part of it was that Edith Morriston, the very last woman he would have suspected of consenting to such a course, who had professed an absolute dislike and repugnance to Henshaw, and fear of his annoying presence, should be meeting him thus willingly. Had he not seen them with his own eyes he would have scoffed at the idea as something inconceivable.

Now what was he to do? For it was clear that, justified or not as he might be thought in interfering in matters which did not concern him, something must be done. The one obvious course which it seemed he ought to take was to give Richard Morriston a hint of what was on foot, if not a stronger and more explicit statement. For that Morriston could be privy to the correspondence between his sister and Henshaw was quite unlikely. If anything underhand was going on, if Henshaw was holding some threat over the girl or pursuing her with unwelcome attentions her brother, as her natural guardian, should be warned. That seemed to Gifford his manifest duty. And yet he shrank from anything which might seem treachery towards the girl. For, if she needed her brother's help and protection against the man, it would be an easy matter for her to complain of his persecution. Why, he wondered, had she not done so? It was all very mysterious. He tried to imagine how the position had come about. On Henshaw's side it was plain enough. Miss Morriston was not only a strikingly handsome girl, but she was an heiress, possessing, according to Kelson, a considerable fortune in her own right. There, clearly, was Henshaw's motive; an incentive to an unscrupulous man to use every art, fair and unfair, to force himself into her favour. But how had he succeeded so quickly as to make this rather haughty, reserved girl consent to meet in secret the man whom she professed to dislike and avoid? That this unpleasantly sharp, pushing product of the less dignified side of the law could have any personal attraction for one of Edith Morriston's taste and discrimination was impossible. And yet there the challenging fact remained that confidential relations had been established between the disparate pair. Was it possible that this man could have found out something connecting Edith Morriston with his brother's death? The feasibility of the idea came as a shock to Gifford. He stopped dead in his walk as the notion took form in his brain. The possibilities of this most mysterious case were too complicated to be grasped at once. And so with his mind in a whirl of vague conjecture and apprehension he reached his hotel. And there a new development in the mystery   awaited   him.

15
ANOTHER DISCOVERY

Kelson was in their sitting-room reading the *Field*. He started up as Gifford entered, and flung away the paper. "My dear Hugh, I've been waiting for you," he exclaimed.

"What's the matter? Anything wrong?" Gifford asked with a certain apprehensive curiosity, as he noticed signs of suppressed excitement in his friend's face.

"I don't know whether it's all wrong or whether it is all right," Kelson replied. "Anyhow it has relieved my mind a good deal."

Controlling his own tendency to excitement, Gifford put aside his hat and stick and sat down. "Let's hear it," he said quietly.

"Well, another unaccountable thing has, it appears, happened at Wynford Place. A pendant, or whatever you call it, to that which has been troubling Muriel. What do you think? As I was riding along the Loxford road this afternoon I met Dick Morriston, and he told me that another discovery of blood-stains has been made at Wynford. On a girl's ball-dress too. And on whose do you suppose it is?"

"Not Miss Morriston's?" Gifford suggested breathlessly.

Kelson nodded, with a slight look of surprise at the correctness of the guess. "Yes. Isn't it queer? Poor old Dick is in rather a way about it, and I must say the whole business is decidedly mysterious."

Gifford was thinking keenly. "How did it come out? Who found the marks?" he asked.

"Well," Kelson answered, "it appears that Edith Morriston's maid found them some days ago, in fact the day after a similar discovery had been made on Muriel's gown. She had brought the dress which her mistress had worn at the Hunt Ball out of the wardrobe where it hung, in order to fold it away. She appears to have spread it on the bed where the sun shone on it and in the strong light she noticed on the dark material some brownish discolorations. With what had happened about the other dress in her mind, she examined the marks closely, and with such intentness as to raise the curiosity of a housemaid who happened to come into the room. At first Miss Morriston's maid tried to put her off, but the other girl, who was sharp-eyed, had seen the marks, was not to be hood-winked, and the mischief was done. The housemaid seems to be a foolish, babbling creature, and the discovery soon became the talk of the servants' hall, whence it spread till it reached the police."

"And what are they doing about it?" Gifford asked.

"Morriston says they've had a detective up at the house examining the gown; being so utterly at sea over the affair the police are doubtless glad to catch at anything. There seems little question that the stains are blood, and that makes the whole business still more puzzling. Dick Morriston is naturally very exercised about it, but I am very glad for Muriel's sake that the second discovery has been made. In fact I have been just waiting till I saw you before riding over to tell her of it, and relieve her mind."

"Yes," Gifford responded mechanically, "of course it removes any serious suspicion from Miss Tredworth."

"And," said Kelson eagerly, "it divides the odium, if there is any. In fact, to my mind, it reduces the whole suspicion to an absurdity. For that both girls could have been concerned in Henshaw's death is absolutely incredible."

"Yes," Gifford agreed thoughtfully; "they could not both have had a hand in it."

"Or either, for that matter," Kelson returned with a laugh. "Don't you admit that the idea is in the highest degree ridiculous?" he added more sharply as Gifford remained silent.

"It is—inconceivable," he admitted abstractedly.

Kelson, who had taken up his hat and crop and was turning to the door, wheeled round quickly. "My dear Hugh," he exclaimed impatiently, "what is the matter with you? What monstrous idea have you got in your head? You owe it to me, and I really must ask you, to speak out plainly. It seems almost an insult to Muriel to ask the question, but do you still persist in the notion that she had, even in the most innocent way, anything to do with Henshaw's death? Because I have her positive assurance that she knows nothing of it, beyond what is common knowledge."

"I too am quite certain of that now," Gifford answered.

"Why do you say now?" Kelson demanded sourly. "Surely you never seriously entertained such an abominable idea."

"You must admit, my dear Harry," Gifford replied calmly, "that with a man stabbed to death in practically the next room, the blood-stains on Miss Tredworth's dress were bound to give rise to conjecture. One would suspect an archbishop in a similar position. But that is all over now. I am as convinced as you can be that Miss Tredworth knew nothing of the business."

"On your honour that is your opinion?"

"On my honour."

"This new discovery has changed your opinion?"

"It has at least shown me how dangerous it may be to jump to conclusions."

Kelson drew in a breath. "Yes, indeed. Poor Muriel has suffered from the suspicion as well as from the horrible shock of the discovery. Still, this new development, though it acquits her, does nothing towards solving the mystery. I wonder whether Edith Morriston has any idea as to how her dress got marked."

"I wonder," Gifford responded abstractedly.

"Well," said Kelson, "I'm off to carry the good news to Muriel. Don't wait dinner for me if I'm not back by seven-thirty."

It was rather a relief to Gifford to be left alone that he might review the situation without interruption. His first thought had been, could this last discovery be accountable for what he had seen that afternoon? Doubtless, after the information reached the police it would not be long in being conveyed to Henshaw. And he was now making use of it to put the screw on, using the hold he had gained over Edith Morriston to bend her to his will. What was that? Marriage? To Gifford the thought was monstrous; yet if it should be that Henshaw had information which put the girl in his power, what could she do? That she had consented to meet him secretly and listen to him went to show that she felt her position to be weak. If so she might need help, an adviser, a man to stand between her and her persecutor.

Thinking out the situation strenuously Gifford determined to seek a private interview with Edith Morriston and offer himself as her protector. At the worst she could but snub him, and the chances were, he thought, greatly in favour of her accepting his offer of help. For from her character he judged she was not a girl to make a stronger appeal to him than the casual invoking of his assistance which had already taken place. He had a very cogent reason for believing that he could be of assistance, although there were certain elements in the mystery which might, in his ignorance of them, upset his calculations.

Anyhow in consideration of the trust Edith Morriston had shown in him he would seek an interview with her and chance what it might bring forth.

16
AN EXPLANATION

In pursuance of this plan Gifford proposed to his friend that they should call at Wynford Place on the next day. Kelson had returned from the Tredworths in high spirits, the news he carried there having lifted a weight off his fiancée's mind and indeed restored the happiness of the whole family. There was no cloud over the engagement now, and they could all look forward to the marriage without a qualm.

If Kelson might, in ordinary circumstances, have wondered at the motive for his friend's proposal, which was but thinly disguised, he was in too happy a state of preoccupation to trouble his head about it.

"I'm your man," he responded promptly. "It so happens that Muriel is lunching at Wynford to-morrow, so it will suit me well enough. I shouldn't be surprised if we get a note in the morning asking us to lunch there too."

The morning, however, brought no note of invitation; a failure which rather surprised Kelson, although Gifford thought he could account for it.

Nevertheless he determined to go and do his best to get a private talk with Edith Morriston, however disinclined she might be to grant it. The two men went up to Wynford early in the afternoon, but it was a long time before Gifford got the opportunity he sought. Edith Morriston seemed as friendly and gracious as ever, but whether by accident or design she gave no chance for Gifford to get in a private word. With the knowledge of what he had seen on the previous afternoon and of the change in her attitude he was too shrewd to show any anxiety for a confidential talk. He watched her closely

when he could do so unobserved, but her face gave no sign
of trouble or embarrassment. He wondered if there could
after all be anything in his idea of persecution, and the
more curious he became the more determined he grew to
find out. But somehow Miss Morriston contrived that
they should never be alone together; when Kelson and
Muriel Tredworth strolled off lover-like, Miss Morriston
kept her brother with her to make a third.

The three went round to the stables and inspected the
hunters, then through the shrubbery to admire a
wonderful bed of snowdrops. As they stood there looking
over the undulating park, and Gifford, curbing his
impatience, was talking of certain changes which had
taken place since his early days there, the butler was
seen hurrying towards them.

"Callers, I suppose," Morriston observed with a half-
yawn. "What is it, Stent?"

"Could I speak to you, sir?" the man said, stopping
short a little distance away.

Morriston went forward to him, and after they had
spoken together he turned round, and with an "Excuse
me for a few minutes," went off towards the house with
the butler.

So at last the opportunity had come. Gifford glanced
at his companion and noticed that her face had gone a
shade paler than before the interruption.

"I wonder what can be the matter," she observed, a
little anxiously Gifford thought. Then she laughed. "I
dare say it is nothing; Stent is becoming absurdly fussy;
and all the alarms and discoveries we have had lately
have not diminished the tendency."

"The latest discovery must have come rather as a
relief," Gifford ventured tentatively.

"The marks on my dress you mean?" She laughed. "So
far that I now share with Muriel Tredworth the suspicion
of knowing all about the tragedy."

"Hardly that," Gifford replied with a smile. "There can
be no cause for that fear. By the way," he added more

seriously, "I owe you an account of my failure to gain any information for you with regard to Mr. Gervase Henshaw's plans."

"He is not communicative?" Miss Morriston suggested casually.

Gifford shook his head. "No, I am never able to get hold of him. In fact, it seems as though he rather makes a point of avoiding us. And if we do meet, he is vagueness and reticence personified."

They were walking slowly back along the shrubbery path. The girl turned to him for an instant, her expression softened in a look of gratitude. "It is very kind of you, Mr. Gifford, to take all this trouble for us. And I am sure it is not your fault that the result is not what you might wish. It was rather absurd of me to set you the task. But I am none the less grateful. Please think that, and do not bother about it anymore."

"But if the man is likely to annoy you," he urged. "Have you longer any reason to fear him?"

She turned swiftly. "Fear him? What do you mean?"

"We thought he might be unscrupulous and might make himself objectionable."

She shrugged. "I dare say it is possible."

"I must confess," he pursued, "I can't quite make the fellow out. Nor his motive for remaining in the place. Your brother told me he came across him hanging about in one of your plantations."

He thought the blood left her face for an instant, but otherwise she showed no sign of discomposure.

"How did he account for his being there?" she asked calmly.

"Unsatisfactorily enough. I forget his actual excuse."

"Was that all?" she demanded coldly.

"I believe so. But it is hardly desirable, as your brother said, to have the man prowling about the property."

For a moment she was silent. "No," she said as though by an afterthought.

Her manner troubled him. "I hope he is not attempting to annoy you," he said searchingly.

She looked surprised and, he thought, a little resentful at his question. "Me?" she returned coldly. "By hanging about in the plantation?"

"If he goes no farther than that—"

"Why should he?" she demanded in the same rather chilling tone.

"I don't know," Gifford replied, set back by her manner. "Except that I have no high opinion of the fellow. It occurred to me he might possibly attempt to persecute you."

She glanced round at him curiously with a little disdainful smile. "What makes you think he would do that?" she returned.

Her attitude was to him not convincing. He felt there was a certain reservation beneath the rather cutting tone. "I am glad to know there is no question of that," he replied with quiet earnestness. "I hope if anything of the kind should occur and you should need a friend you will not overlook me."

"You are very kind," she responded, but without turning towards him. He thought, however, that her low tone had softened, and it gave him hope.

"I should scarcely take upon myself to suggest this," he said, "but I am emboldened by two facts. One that you have already asked me to be your ally, your friend, in this business, the other that there is something about Henshaw and his actions which I do not understand. I hope you will forgive my boldness."

His companion had glanced round now, keenly, as though to probe for the meaning which might lie beneath his words. He speculated whether she might be wondering how much he knew; was he cognisant of her meeting with Henshaw?

But, whatever her thought, she answered in the same even voice, "There is nothing to forgive. On the contrary I am most grateful."

They were nearing the house, and Gifford was debating whether he dared suggest another turn along the shrubbery path, when Richard Morriston appeared at the hall door, beckoned to them, and went in again.

"I wonder what Dick wants. Has anything more come to light?" Miss Morriston observed with a rather bored laugh as she slightly quickened her pace.

As they went in she called, "Dick!" and he answered her from the library. There they found him with Kelson and Muriel Tredworth. A glance at their faces told Gifford that they were all in a state of scarcely suppressed excitement.

"I say, Edith, what do you think?" her brother exclaimed. "We've made a rather important discovery. Were you in the middle room of the tower during the dance?"

For a moment his sister did not answer.

"No; I don't think I was," she said, with what seemed to Gifford a certain amount of apprehension in her eyes, although her expression was calm enough.

"Oh, but, my dear girl, you must have been," Morriston insisted vehemently. "We have found the explanation of the stains on Miss Tredworth's dress and on yours."

"You have?" his sister replied, looking at him curiously.

"Yes; beyond all doubt. The mystery is made clear. Come and see."

He led the way across the hall and up the first story of the tower. "There's the explanation," he said, pointing to some dark red patches on the back of a sofa and on the carpet below.

"It is not a pleasant idea," Morriston said; "but you see these marks are directly under the place where the dead man lay in the room above. The blood from his wound evidently ran through the chinks of the flooring on to the beams of the ceiling here and so fell drop by drop on the couch and on any one sitting there. Rather gruesome, but I am sure we must be all very glad to get the simple explanation. The only wonder is that no one thought of it before."

"Muriel was sitting just at that end of the sofa when I proposed to her," Kelson said in a low voice to Gifford.

"I am delighted the matter is so completely accounted for," his friend returned. "What fools we were ever to have taken it so tragically."

But his expression changed as he glanced at Edith Morriston; she had denied that she had been in the room.

"I have sent down to the police to tell them of the discovery," Morriston was saying. "The fact is that since the tragedy the servants appear to have rather shunned this part of the house, or at any rate to have devoted as little time to it as possible. Otherwise this would have come to light sooner. Anyhow it is a source of congratulation to Miss Tredworth and you, Edith. Of course you must have been in here."

"I remember sitting just there; ugh!" Miss Tredworth said with a shudder.

"I can swear to that," Kelson corroborated with a knowing smile.

"You must have done the same or brushed against the sofa, Edith," Morriston said cheerfully. "Well, I'm glad that's settled, although it brings us no nearer towards solving the mystery of what happened overhead."

"No," Kelson remarked. "It looks as though that was going to remain a mystery."

The butler came in. "Major Freeman is here, sir," he said, "with Mr. Henshaw, and would like to speak to you."

Morriston looked surprised. "Alfred has been very quick. We sent him off only about a quarter of an hour ago."

"Alfred met Major Freeman and Mr. Henshaw with the detective just beyond the lodge gates, sir."

"Then they were coming up here independently of my message?"

"Yes, sir. Alfred gave Major Freeman the message and came back."

Morriston moved towards the door. "I will see these gentlemen at once," he said.

"In the library, sir."

Involuntarily Gifford had glanced at Edith Morriston. She was standing impassively with set face; and at his glance she turned away to the window. But not before he had caught in her eyes a look which he hated to see, a look which seemed to confirm a suspicion already in his mind.

17
WHAT A GIRL SAW

With Morriston's departure a rather uncomfortable silence fell upon the party left in the room. Everyone seemed to feel that there was something in the air, the shadow of a possibly serious development in the case. Even Kelson, who was otherwise inclined to be jubilant over the freeing of his fiancée from suspicion, seemed to feel it was no time or place just then for gaiety, and his expression grew as grave as that of the rest.

"I wonder what these fellows have come to say," he observed as he paced the room.

"Let's hope to announce that at last they are going to leave you in peace, Edith," Miss Tredworth said.

Edith Morriston did not alter her position as she stood looking out of the window. "Thank you for your kind wish, Muriel," she responded in a cold voice; "but I'm afraid that is too much to hope for just yet."

"Yet one doesn't see what else it can be," Kelson observed reflectively. "They can hardly have found out exactly how the man came by his death; much more likely to have abandoned their latest theory, eh, Hugh?"

Gifford was looking, held by the grip of his imagination, at the tall figure by the window; wondering what was passing behind that veil of impassiveness. "I don't see what they can have found out away from this house," he said, rousing himself by an effort to answer; "and they don't seem to have been here lately."

"Well, we shall see," Kelson said casually. "Ah, here comes Dick back again."

Morriston hurried in with a serious face. In answer to Kelson's, "Well, Dick?" he said.

"It appears a rather extraordinary piece of evidence has just come to light; one which, if true, completely solves the mystery of the locked door. I asked Freeman if there was any objection to you fellows coming to the library and hearing the story; he is quite agreeable. So will you come? You too, Edith, and Miss Tredworth; there is nothing at all horrible in it so far."

For the first time Edith Morriston turned from the window. "Is it necessary, Dick?" she protested quietly. "I'd just as soon hear it all afterwards from you. These police visitations are rather getting on my nerves."

"Very well, dear; you shall hear all about it later on," her brother responded, and led the way down to the library. Gifford was the last to leave the room, and his glance back showed him that Edith Morriston had turned again to the window and resumed her former attitude.

In the library were the chief constable, Gervase Henshaw and a local detective.

"Now, Major Freeman," Morriston said as he closed the door, "we shall be glad to hear this new piece of evidence."

Major Freeman bowed. "Shortly, it comes to this," he began. "A young woman named Martha Haynes, belonging to Branchester, called at my office this morning and made a statement which, if reliable, must have an important bearing on this mysterious case.

"It appears from her story that on the night of the Hunt Ball held here she had been paying a visit to some friends at Rapscot, a village, as you know, about a mile beyond Wynford. On her way back to the town, for which she started at about 9.45, she took as a short cut the right-of-way path running across the park and passing near the house. As she went by she was naturally attracted by the lighted windows and could hear the band quite plainly. She stopped to listen to the music at a point which she has indicated, almost directly opposite the tower.

"She says she had stood there for some little time when her attention was suddenly diverted to what seemed a mysterious movement on the outside of the tower. A dark body, presumably a human being, appeared to be slowly sliding down the wall from the topmost window. Unfortunately before she could quite realize what she was looking at—and we may imagine that a country girl would take some little time to grasp so unusual a situation—a cloud drifted across the moon and threw the tower into shadow.

"The girl continued, however, to keep her eyes fixed on the spot where she had seen the dark object descending, with the result that in a few seconds she saw it reach and pass over one side of the window of the lower room which was sufficiently lighted up to silhouette anything placed before it. She saw the object move slowly over the window and disappear in the darkness beneath it. When, a few seconds later, the moon came out again nothing more was to be seen.

"The girl stayed for some time watching the tower, but without result. She is a more or less ignorant, unsophisticated country-woman, and what she had seen she was quite unable to account for. Naturally she hardly connected it with any sort of tragical occurrence. The house with its lights and music seemed given over to gaiety; that any one should just then have met his death in that upper room never entered her imagination. A vague idea that a thief might have got into the house and she had seen him escape by the tower window did indeed, as she says, cross her mind, and that supposition prevented her from approaching the tower to satisfy her curiosity. But as nothing more happened she began to think less of the significance of what she had seen, in fact almost persuaded herself that it had been something of an optical delusion. Presently, having had enough of standing in the cold wind, she resumed her way, went home and to bed, and early next morning left the town to enter a situation in another part of the country.

"It appears that she had taken cold by her loitering and soon after reaching her destination became so ill that she had to keep her bed, and it was only on her recovery a few days ago that she heard what had happened here that night. Directly she could get away she came over and told her story to us."

"A pity she could not have come before," Morriston remarked as the chief constable paused. "Her evidence is highly important, disposing as it does of the mystery of the locked door."

"Yes," Major Freeman agreed, "and also of the suicide theory. The question now is—who was the person who was seen descending from the window?"

"Could this girl tell whether it was a man or a woman?" The question came from Henshaw, who had hitherto kept silent.

"She thinks it was a man," Major Freeman answered, "but could not swear to it. The fact of the object being close to the wall made it almost impossible in the imperfect light to distinguish plainly. But I think we may take it that it was a man. The feat could be hardly one a woman would undertake."

"No," Gifford agreed. "And there would seem little chance of identifying the person."

"None at all so far as the girl Haynes is concerned," Major Freeman replied. "But we have something to go upon; a starting point for a new line of inquiry. The person seen escaping must have lowered himself by a rope from that top window and a considerable length would be required. I have taken the liberty, Mr. Morriston, of setting a party of my men to search the grounds for the rope; they will begin by dragging the little lake."

"By all means," Morriston assented.

"Detective Sprules," the chief proceeded, "would like to make another examination of the ironwork of the window. May he go up now?"

"Certainly," Morriston answered, and the detective left the room.

Gifford spoke. "The girl saw nothing of the escaping person after he reached the ground?"

"Nothing, she says," Major Freeman answered. "But the base of the tower was in deep shadow, which would prevent that."

"A pity her curiosity was not a little more practical," Henshaw observed.

"Yes." Gifford turned to him. "You are proved correct, Mr. Henshaw, in your repudiation of the suicide idea. Perhaps, in view of this latest development, you may have knowledge to go upon of someone from whom your brother might have apprehended danger?"

Henshaw's set face gave indication of nothing but a studied reserve. "No one certainly," he answered coolly, "from whom he might apprehend danger to his life."

"There must have been a motive for the act," Kelson observed. "Unless it was a sudden quarrel."

"There appears," Major Freeman put in, "to be no evidence whatever of anything leading up to that."

"No; the cause is so far quite mysterious," Henshaw said.

It seemed to Gifford that there was something of undisclosed knowledge behind his words, and he fell to wondering how far the motive was mysterious to him.

Morriston proceeded to acquaint Major Freeman with the discovered cause of the marks on the ladies' dresses, and they all went off to the lower room where the position of the stains was pointed out. Edith Morriston was no longer there.

"Miss Tredworth sat at this end of the sofa," Morriston explained, "and so the marks on her dress are clearly accounted for."

"And Miss Morriston?" Henshaw put the question in a tone which had in it, Gifford thought, a touch of scepticism.

"Oh, my sister must have been in here too," Morriston replied. "Or how could her dress have been stained? Unless, indeed, she brushed against Miss Tredworth's or someone else's. That's clear."

There seemed no alacrity in Henshaw to accept the conclusion and he did not respond.

"I am glad this part of the mystery is so satisfactorily settled," the chief constable remarked. "Now we have the issue narrowed. Well, Sprules?"

The detective had appeared at the door.

"I have examined the ironwork of the window, sir," he said, "and have found under the magnifying-glass traces of the fraying of a rope as though caused by friction against the iron staple."

"Sufficient signs to bear out the young woman's statement?"

"Quite, sir. There is upon close examination distinct evidence of a rope having been worked against the hinge of the window."

"Very good, Sprules. We may consider that point settled," Major Freeman said.

Having finally satisfied themselves as to the cause of the stains on the floor and sofa, the chief constable and his subordinate proposed to go to the lake and see whether the men who were dragging it had had any success. Morriston and Henshaw with Kelson and Gifford accompanied them. As they came in sight of the boat the detective exclaimed, "They have found it!" and the men were seen hauling up a rope out of the water.

"Sooner than I expected," Major Freeman observed as they hurried towards the nearest point to the boat.

The rope when landed proved to be of considerable length, sufficient when doubled, they calculated, to reach from the topmost window to within five or six feet of the ground.

"The escaping person," Henshaw said, "must have slid down the doubled rope which had been passed through the staple of the window, and then when the ground was reached have pulled it away, coiled it up, carried it to the lake, and thrown it in. Obviously that was the procedure and it accounts completely for the locked door."

The chief constable and the detective agreed.

"A man would want some nerve to come down from that height," the latter remarked.

"Any man, or woman either for that matter," Henshaw returned dogmatically, "would not hesitate to take the risk as an alternative to being trapped up there with his victim."

"You are not suggesting it might have been a woman who was seen sliding down the rope?" Gifford asked pointedly.

Henshaw shrugged. "I suggest nothing as to the person's identity," he replied in a sharply guarded tone. "That is now what remains to be discovered."

18
THE LOST BROOCH

The police authorities with Henshaw and Morriston went off with the rope to experiment in the room of the tragedy.

"I don't suppose we are wanted," Kelson said quietly to Gifford; "let's go for a turn round the garden. I wonder where Muriel has got to."

They found Miss Tredworth on the lawn. "I am waiting for Edith," she said.

"We'll stroll on and Gifford can bring Miss Morriston after us," Kelson suggested, and the lovers moved away, leaving Gifford, much to his satisfaction, waiting for Edith Morriston.

In a few minutes she made her appearance. Gifford mentioned the arrangement and they strolled off by the path the others had taken.

It seemed to Gifford that his companion's manner was rather abnormal; unlike her usual cold reserve there were signs of a certain suppressed excitement.

"I hope," she said, "that Major Freeman and his people are satisfied with our discovery that the marks on Muriel's dress and mine came there by accident."

"Evidently quite convinced," Gifford answered.

"That's well," she responded with a rather forced laugh. "It was rather too bad to suspect us, on that evidence, of knowing anything about the affair."

"I don't suppose for a moment they did," Gifford assured her.

"I don't know," the girl returned. "Anyhow it was rather an embarrassing, not to say painful, position for us to be in. But that is at an end now."

Nevertheless Gifford could tell that she was not so thoroughly relieved as her words implied.

"Completely," he declared. "You have heard of the new piece of evidence?" he added casually.

For a moment she stopped with a start, instantly recovering herself. "No; what is that?" in a tone almost of unconcern.

Gifford told her of the statement made by the country girl and its corroboration in the finding of the rope. As he continued he felt sure that the story was gripping his companion more and more closely. At last she stopped dead and turned to him with eyes which had in them intense mystification as well as fear.

"Mr. Gifford, do you believe that story?"

"I see no reason for disbelieving it," he answered quietly. "It is practically the only conceivable solution of the mystery of the locked door."

"Surely–" she stopped, checking the vehement objection that rose to her lips. "This girl," she went on as though searching for a plausible argument, "is it not likely that she was mistaken? We know what these country people are. And she could not have seen very clearly."

"But," Gifford argued gently, "her statement is confirmed by the finding of the rope."

Edith Morriston was thinking strenuously, desperately, he could see that. The words she spoke were but mechanical, the mere froth of a seething brain. Yet her splendid self-command–and he recognized it with admiration–never deserted her, however supreme the struggle may have been to retain it.

A seat was by them; she went across the path to it and sat down. Gifford saw that she was deadly pale.

"I fear this wretched business is upsetting you, Miss Morriston," he said gently. "Let me run to the house and fetch something to revive you."

She made a gesture to stay him, and by an effort seemed to shake off the threatening collapse. "No, no," she said; "please don't. It is very stupid of me, but these repeated shocks are rather trying. You see one has never had any experience of the sort before."

"It was more than stupid of me to blunder into the story," Gifford said self-reproachfully. "But it never occurred to me—"

"No, no; of course not," she responded. "And, after all, I am bound to hear all about it sooner or later. Sit down and tell me your opinion of the affair. Supposing the girl was not mistaken who do you think the person seen escaping from the window could have been?"

"That is difficult to say."

"A thief, no doubt."

"That is a natural conclusion."

"Have the police any idea?"

"Not that I know of. I should say decidedly no definite idea."

"Or Mr. Henshaw?"

"Whatever Mr. Henshaw's ideas may be he keeps them to himself."

Miss Morriston checked the remark she had seemed about to make, and for a few minutes there was an awkward silence. Gifford broke it.

"I am so sorry that I have been unable to get any hint of his intentions. Believe me, it has not been for want of trying. But the man, for reasons best known to himself, seems determined to remain inscrutable."

The girl was staring in front of her. "Yes," she responded, with a catch of her breath; "that is evident. But it does not much matter. I know you have tried your best to do what I was foolish enough to ask you. And now please do not think any more of it. In my ignorance of the man's character I set you an impossible task. All I can do now is to thank you for your sympathy and devotion."

Her tone pained him horribly. "I hope, Miss Morriston," he replied warmly, "you are not asking me to end my devotion."

She gave a little bitter laugh. "Seeing that it is useless I have no right to ask its continuance," she replied almost coldly, "nor to expect you to involve yourself in my–in our worries."

"But if I ask to be allowed that privilege?" he urged.

She shook her head. "No, no, my friend," she insisted, with less warmth than the words implied, "it can lead to no good and would be a mistake. Let the man alone. To involve yourself with him can bring you nothing but trouble. Promise me you will take no further heed of this unhappy business."

She turned to him as she spoke the last words, and there seemed less trouble in her face than in his. For at his heart there was a sickening fear and suspicion of what the words portended.

"I can't promise that," he objected.

"But I ask you; it is my wish," she returned with a touch of command.

"For my sake, or yours?" he rejoined.

"For both. Give me your promise. You must if we are to remain friends."

Her look and the fascination in her voice seemed to pull the very heart out of him.

"You are asking a cruelly hard thing of me," he replied, with a tremor in his voice. "I don't understand–"

"No, you don't understand," she interrupted quickly. "It is enough to know that you have taken a girl's foolish commission too seriously, so seriously as to run the risk of making things even worse than they threatened to be. Now I ask you to leave well alone."

"If it is well," he said doubtfully.

"Of course. Why should it not be?" she rejoined, in a not very convincing tone. "Now I shall rely on you–and I am sure it will not be in vain–to respect my wishes. Things seem to be in a horrible muddle," she added with a rather dreary laugh, "but let's hope they will right themselves before long."

She rose, compelling him to rise too. Something in the tone and manner of her last speech made him quite unwilling to end their conference, and desperately anxious to speak out everything that was in his mind and try to bring matters to a crisis.

"Don't go for a moment," he said as she began to move away towards the house. "I have something to say to you."

She turned quickly and faced him with a suggestion of displeasure in her eyes. "What is it?" she said with a touch of impatience.

"Only this," he answered quietly. "Have you lost a brooch, Miss Morriston?"

At the question the blood left her cheeks as it had done a little while before; then surged back till her face was suffused.

"A brooch? Yes; I have missed one. Have you found it?" The words were spoken with a calmness which failed to hide the eagerness behind them.

"I think so," he answered, taking out his letter-case. "A pearl, set in diamonds mounted on a safety-pin?"

He opened the case and showed it pinned into the soft lining.

"Yes; that is mine," she said; and for a moment or two by a strange attraction each looked into the other's eyes.

Gifford bent his head over the case as he unfastened the brooch and took it out.

"Where–where did you find it?" Something in the girl's voice made him glad that he was not looking at her.

"In the garden," he said.

"In the garden?" she repeated. He was looking up now and saw the intense relief in her face. "To-day?"

"No; last time I was up here. I ought to have taken it to the house at once but–but it was a temptation to me to keep it till I could give it back to you like this. Do forgive me."

It was plain she divined what he meant, but her cold manner came to the aid of her embarrassment.

"I am only too glad to have it again. I am so glad you found it."

"So am I," he responded with a touch of fervour. "I wish I could relieve your mind of everything else as easily."

"I am sure you do," she said wistfully, and impulsively half put out her hand.

He caught it as she was in the act of checking the action and drawing it back. "You may be sure–quite sure, of my devotion," he said, and raised her hand to his lips.

An exclamation and a sudden start as the hand was quickly withdrawn made him look up. Edith Morriston's eyes were fixed with something like fear on an object behind him. An intuition told him what it was before he looked round to see Henshaw, with his characteristic, rather stealthy walk, coming towards them.

Gifford set his teeth hard as the two faced round and awaited Henshaw's approach.

"This man shall not annoy you," he said in an undertone.

"Don't quarrel with him, for heaven's sake," she entreated in the same tone, under her breath, as the disturbing presence drew near. There was a strange excitement in her voice, though none in the set face.

"I think your brother is looking for you, Miss Morriston," Henshaw said in his even voice when he was within a dozen paces of them.

"I was just going to look for him," the girl replied in a voice strangely changed from that in which she had talked with Gifford. "Isn't it lucky? Mr. Gifford has picked up in the garden a brooch I lost some days ago. I did not dare to tell Dick, as it was his gift."

Henshaw gave a casual glance at the ornament. "I congratulate you," he responded coolly. Then Gifford saw his eyes seek hers as he added: "Where was it found? Near the tower?"

The covert malice of the insinuation was plain in the questioner's look, although the tone was casual enough.

"No. On the lawn," Gifford replied quietly.

19
IN THE CHURCHYARD

Nothing more of importance happened that day at Wynford, and Gifford had no further opportunity of private talk with Edith Morriston. But it was evident to him, and the knowledge gave him intense concern, that the girl went in fear of Gervase Henshaw. That he was intimidating her, and using his brother's death for that purpose, was beyond doubt, and the very fact that Edith Morriston was a woman of uncommon courage and self-control, one who in ordinary circumstances would be the last to give way to fear or submit to bullying, showed how serious the matter had become.

Gifford on his part determined that this intolerable state of things must come to an end, and that in spite of the command laid upon him by the girl, he would now pit himself against her persecutor. He had given no actual promise, and even if he had it would have been drawn from him in ignorance of certain means which he possessed of help in this crisis.

And a significant circumstance which came to Gifford's knowledge a day or two after his interview with Edith Morriston in the garden of Wynford, was the cause of his beginning to take action without further delay.

Late on the next Sunday afternoon Gifford had gone for a country walk which he had arranged to bring him round in time for the evening service at the little village church of Wynford standing just outside the park boundary. His way took him by well-remembered field-paths which, although towards the end of his walk darkness had set in, he had no difficulty in tracing. The last field he crossed brought him to a by-road joining the highway which ran through Wynford, the junction being about a quarter of a mile from the church. As he neared the stile which admitted to the road he saw, on the other side of the hedge and showing just above it, the head of a man. At the sound of his footsteps the man quickly turned, and, as for a moment the fitful moonlight caught his face, Gifford was sure he recognized Gervase Henshaw. But he took no notice and kept on his way to the stile, which he crossed and gained the road. As he did so he glanced back. A horse and trap was waiting there with Henshaw in it. He was now bending down, probably with the object of concealing his identity, and had moved on a few paces farther down the road.

Why was he waiting there? Gifford asked himself the obvious question with a decidedly uneasy feeling. Henshaw the Londoner, on a Sunday evening, waiting with a horse and trap in an unfrequented lane, a road which ran nowhere but to a farm. What did it mean?

Naturally Gifford's suspicions connected Edith Morriston with the circumstance, and yet he told himself the idea was monstrously improbable. It was more likely that Henshaw was bound upon some search with the police. His movements were and had been for some time mysterious enough.

Gifford's impulse as he turned into the high road was to stay there in concealment and watch for the upshot of Henshaw's presence. The suggestion did not, however, altogether commend itself to him. He disliked the idea of spying even upon such a man as Henshaw, whom he had good reason to suspect of playing a dastardly game. It was probable, too, that Henshaw had recognized him and might be on the look-out; it would be intensely humiliating to be caught watching. So, turning the pros and cons over in his mind, Gifford walked slowly on in a state of irresolution till he came to a wicket-gate which admitted from the road to a path which ran through the churchyard.

There he stopped, debating with himself whether he should turn back and keep an eye on Henshaw or go on into the church where service was just beginning. It did seem absurd to imagine that Henshaw with his conveyance could be waiting there by appointment for a girl of the character and position of Edith Morriston. True, he had seen them walking together in secret, which was strange enough, but that need not necessarily have been a planned meeting.

Such an urgent curiosity had hold of him at the bare possibility of something wrong that he, temporizing with his scruples, was about to turn back to the lane, when he saw the figure of a woman coming towards him along the churchyard path. She was tall and so far as he could make out, muffled in a cloak and veil. His heart gave a leap, for although the woman's face and figure were indistinguishable the height and gait corresponded with those of Edith Morriston.

As she came near the little gate where he stood she stopped dead, seemed to hesitate a moment, and then turned as though to go back. Determined to set his doubts at rest Gifford passed quickly through the gate and followed her at an overtaking pace. Evidently sensible of her pursuit, the woman quickened her steps and, as Gifford gained on her, turned quickly from the path, threading her way among the graves to escape him. She had gone but a few steps when in her hurry she tripped over the mound of a small, unmarked grave and fell to the ground.

Gifford ran to her and taking her arm assisted her to rise.

"Miss Morriston!" he exclaimed, for he now was sure of her identity. "I hope you are not hurt," he added mechanically, his mind full of a greater and more critical contingency.

"Mr. Gifford!" she responded; but he was sure she had not recognized him then for the first time. "Oh, no, thank you; I am not in the least hurt. It was stupid of me to trip and fall like that. Are you going to church?" she added, evidently wishing to get away.

"I was," he answered. "And you?"

"I was too," she said, conquering her embarrassment, "but I have a headache, and prefer the fresh air. Don't let me keep you," she held out her hand. "Service has begun."

He took her hand. "Miss Morriston," he said gravely, "don't think me very unmannerly, but I am not going to leave you here."

In the bright moonlight he could see her expression of rather haughty surprise. "I think you are unmannerly, Mr. Gifford," she retorted defiantly. "May I ask why you are not going to leave me here?"

"Because," he answered with quiet decision, "Mr. Henshaw is waiting just there in Turner's Lane."

"Is he?" The same defiant note; but there was anxiety behind the cold pretence.

"Yes. And pardon me, I have an idea he is waiting there for you."

His firm tone and manner baffled equivocation. "What is it to you if he is?" she returned with a brave attempt to suggest cold displeasure. But her lip trembled and her voice was scarcely steady.

"It is something to me," he replied insistently, "because it means a great deal to you. This man is persecuting you. He is–"

"Mr. Gifford!" she exclaimed. "You take–"

He held up his hand. "Please let me finish, Miss Morriston. I can convince you that I am not taking too much upon myself. I am no fool and am not interfering without warrant. This man Henshaw has succeeded in persuading you that you are in his power. That is very far from being the case, and I can prove it."

"I don't understand you, Mr. Gifford."

The tone of cold annoyance was gone now. Relief and a vague hope seemed to be struggling with an almost overwhelming anxiety.

"You will understand directly," he replied. "I have more than a suspicion that this man is seeking to connect you with his brother's death and is making use of a certain half-knowledge he possesses to get a hold over you. Is that not so?"

For a while she was silent, her breath coming quickly, as she hesitated how to meet the direct question. Gifford hated, yet somehow rejoiced, to see this proud, cold-mannered girl brought to this pass, and the reason he rejoiced lay in the knowledge that he could help her out of it.

At length she spoke. "Mr. Gifford, I trust you as a man of honour. Your conjecture is right, but unhappily there is no help for it."

"There is help," he declared reassuringly. "Can this man prove that you are in any way guilty of his brother's death?"

The girl gave a shiver. "He can by implication," she admitted in a low voice.

"Can he prove it?"

"Not actually, perhaps. But far enough to disgrace me and mine forever," she said with a sob.

"And with that idea he terrorizes you?" The question was put with quiet sternness.

"Yes, yes; but I cannot help it! I cannot bear it. Oh, let me go." She seemed now in an agony of fear.

Gifford laid his hand on her as she sought to move away towards the gate and the waiting enemy.

"Miss Morriston," he said with decision, "you must not go; you must have no more communication with this man Henshaw. He can prove nothing against you, while I can prove everything in your favour."

Her look of fear and impatience changed at the last words to one of startled incredulity.

"You, Mr. Gifford? What do you mean?"

"Exactly what I say," he returned decisively, "I can prove, if need be, that you had no hand in that cowardly ruffian's death."

"You? How?" the girl gasped, staring at him with dilated eyes.

"I will convince you," he answered quietly. "When I told you the other day that I had found your brooch on the lawn I said, for an obvious reason, what was not true. I found it in the room where Clement Henshaw died."

"You did," the girl gasped almost in terror. "When?"

"A few minutes after his death," Gifford replied calmly. "I happened to be present in the room when he came by his fatal wound."

20

An Involuntary Eavesdropper

As she heard the words Edith Morriston stood for a moment as though transfixed, and then staggered back grasping at a tombstone for support. Gifford took a quick step forward, but before he could be of help she had recovered from the shock, and motioning him back, was looking at him with incredulous eyes.

"You were there?" she repeated, with more suspicion now than unbelief.

"In that room at the top of the tower; yes; by accident," he answered in a tone calculated to reassure her.

"Then you know—you saw what happened?"

He bowed his head in assent. "Enough to be sure that Mr. Clement Henshaw was a great scoundrel, and that his fate was not altogether unmerited. Now," he added in a tone of decision, "you will have nothing more to do with this Gervase Henshaw, or he with you."

It was good to see the eager relief in Edith Morriston's eyes.

"And you never told me this before," she said.

"I could not very well," he replied. "And I should not have told you now had I not been forced to protect you from this man. It is a dangerous position for me to stand in, and I should in ordinary circumstances have let the affair remain a mystery."

"I understand your position," she responded, with a look of gratitude. "But you can trust me."

"Indeed I can," he assured her with infinite content.

"I don't realize it now," the girl said, with signs that she was fighting against the effect of the reaction. "Can you trust me enough to tell me how it all happened?"

"I would trust you with my life," he responded fervently. "Though it hardly comes to that. Of course I will tell you the whole story of my adventure. But we had better not stay here. Mr. Henshaw must be getting impatient by this time and may come to look for you. Before he has the chance of meeting you it will be well for you to hear the real facts of the case. Shall we come into the park, or would your brother–"

"Dick is at church," she said, a little shamefacedly, it seemed. "I gave him the slip."

"What a terrible risk you have just run," Gifford observed as they went through the churchyard to the private gate into the park. "If I had not happened to come along just then and see Henshaw waiting–"

"Oh, don't talk of that now," she entreated. "I knew it meant horrible misery for the rest of my life, but anything seemed better than the terrible scandal which threatened us."

"With which Henshaw threatened you, the scoundrel," Gifford corrected. "Now you shall see how little he really had to go upon."

"And yet," she murmured, "it seemed overwhelming. I can scarcely believe even now that the danger is past."

"Wait till you hear my story," he said with a reassuring smile.

They had entered the enclosed path, called Church Walk, and passing the branch which led to the drive, kept on between the tall laurel hedges.

"We shall be quite undisturbed here," the girl said. "Dick is sure to turn off and go in by the drive. Now, Mr. Gifford, do trust me and tell me everything."

"I hope it is not necessary to talk of trust between us," he replied, with as much tenderness as his chivalry permitted.

"No; forgive me; I hope not," she responded quietly. "Now please tell me, Mr. Gifford, what I am longing to hear."

"You will remember," Gifford began, as they slowly paced the moon-lit path, "that on the evening I came down here my suitcase containing my evening clothes had gone astray on the railway. There was no chance of its turning up at the hotel before ten o'clock, and I was therefore prevented from appearing at the dance till quite late. Naturally I would not hear of Kelson waiting for me, which like the good-natured fellow he is, he proposed to do; he therefore went off in good time."

"Yes; I remember he arrived quite early," Edith Morriston murmured.

"Clement Henshaw," Gifford proceeded, "left the hotel about the same time. They must have reached your house within a few minutes of one another."

As he paused, his companion looked round at him inquiringly. "Yes," she said, with a certain suggestion of reticence; "I remember that too."

Gifford continued. "Having seen Kelson off, I went up to our sitting-room to wait till my kit should arrive. I was very keen on seeing again the old place where in my young days I used to spend such happy months, and my enforced waiting soon became almost intolerable boredom. The result was that I got a fit of the fidgets; I could not settle down to read, and at last, having still an hour to spare, I resolved in my restlessness to stroll out and take a preliminary look from outside at what was practically my old home."

"Yes." There was a catch of growing excitement in Edith Morriston's voice, which was scarcely above a whisper.

"The wind was sharp that night, as we all know," Gifford went on, "and forbade loitering. A smart walk of fifteen or twenty minutes brought me here, knowing as I did every path and short cut across the park. The old familiar house looked picturesque enough with its many lighted windows and every sign of gaiety. Keeping away from the front entrance where carriages were constantly driving up and a good many people were about, I went round to the other side, avoiding the stables and passing along by the west wing. This, of course, brought me to the old tower, the scene of many a game and frolic in my young days. At its foot I stood for a while recalling memories of the past. In the mere idleness of affectionate remembrance I went up to the garden door of the tower and mechanically turned the handle. It was unlocked.

"I hardly know what made me go in; an impulse to stand again in those once familiar surroundings. It was fascinating to be in the old tower which the dim light showed me was just as I had last seen it more than a dozen years ago. The past came vividly back to me, and I stood there for a while indulging in a reverie of old days. The associations of the place seemed every moment to grip me more compellingly. The tower seemed quiet and altogether deserted; all I could hear was the dance-music away in the hall. There could be no risk, I thought, of being seen if I went up to the floor above: and I quietly ascended the stairs to the first landing. The narrow passage leading to the hall was lighted up with sconces; at its farther end I could see the movement of the dancers. The band was playing a favourite waltz of mine, and I stayed there rather enjoying the music and the sight from my safe retreat.

"It did not seem likely that anyone would be coming to the tower, and I resolved, foolishly enough, for, of course, I was in my travelling suit, to wander up to the next floor and take a look at the room which held a rather sentimental association for me. It was a stupid thing to do as I was there in, for the moment, a rather questionable situation, still I felt pretty secure from being noticed, and went up warily to the next floor.

"There I found the room considerably altered from my recollection of it, especially as it was arranged as a sitting-out room, but no one was there, nor were there any signs of its having been used, which from its rather secluded position, was natural enough.

"Having given a reminiscent look round I concluded that it would be best to make a retreat, especially as there would be ample opportunity later in the evening for me to visit it again. I turned and went to the door. On reaching the stairs I heard to my great annoyance the sounds of persons coming up and the subdued tones of a man's voice, I realized that I was caught, and my one chance of escape was to retreat up the topmost flight of stairs and wait in the darkness till the couple had gone into the room I had just quitted.

"Accordingly I turned and went up the remaining flight on tip-toe, two stairs at a time, waiting beyond the turn in hiding till the coast should be clear.

"The couple had now reached the landing below and, so far as I could tell, went into the room. I was just about to make a quick descent, hoping to get past that and other awkward points unnoticed, when to my dismay I became aware that the people whom I had thought safely settled in the room below had come out and were beginning to mount the topmost flight of stairs. This was indeed a most awkward predicament for me, and I debated for a moment whether my best course would not be to go boldly down the stairs and pass them, rather than retreat to the top room. If I had chosen the former course how differently things might have turned out; at any rate, for better or worse, the situation as it exists to-day might have presented itself in quite another form."

Edith Morriston glanced quickly at Gifford as he uttered the reflection. She seemed about to speak, but checked the impulse, and he continued:

"Treading noiselessly, I bolted up the remaining stairs and went into the dark room at the top. At the door, which stood open, I stopped and listened. To my intense vexation, for the situation was becoming decidedly unpleasant, the pair were still coming up. In silence now, but I could hear their approaching footsteps and the rustle of the lady's dress. Unfortunately, there was no corner on the top landing where I could stand hidden, so I was forced to draw back into the room.

"Happily it had been so familiar to me from childhood that I could find my way about it in the dark. I well remembered the little inner room formed by the bartizan of the tower, and into this I tip-toed, feeling horribly guilty. If only I had not been in that suspicious brown suit! In evening clothes there would, of course, have been no necessity for this surreptitious retreat. I devoutly hoped that the two were merely bent on exploring the place and that the darkness of the old lumber-room would quickly satisfy their curiosity and send them down again. I heard them come into the room, the man speaking in a tone so low that the words were indistinguishable from where I stood; and then the sound of the door being shut struck my ear unpleasantly.

"Then the man spoke in a more audible voice, a voice which in a flash I recognized as Henshaw's. And his first words caught my attention with an unpleasant grip."

21
GIFFORD CONTINUES HIS STORY

"'Failing to get the regular invitation I had a right to expect, I have had to take this mode of seeing you,' I just caught the words in Henshaw's metallic, rather penetrating voice.

"The lady's reply was given in a tone so low that at the distance I stood the words were indistinguishable.

"'Unmanly?' he exclaimed, evidently taking up her word. 'I don't admit that for a moment. You know how we stand to one another and what my feelings are towards you. It is no use for you to try to ignore them or me. I won't stand being treated like this. There is no reason why my advances should be repulsed as though they were an insult.'

"I caught the last words of the lady's reply: '—good reason, and you know it.'

"It was more than clear to me now that I was to be the witness of a very hateful piece of business. The man's tone, even more than his words, made my blood boil, and I began to congratulate myself on being thus accidentally in a position to protect, if need be, the girl whom this fellow was evidently bullying. With the utmost care I crept nearer to the small curtained arch which admitted to the larger room. The pitch darkness of the little turret chamber in which I stood made me feel quite safe from observation. And I had no qualms now about eavesdropping; the situation surely justified it.

"I went forward till I could get a sight round the arch of the two persons in the room. They were standing near the window at some distance from me. In the obscurity, not quite as impenetrable as that out of which I looked, I could distinguish the tall figure of the girl in a dark ball-dress, and facing her, towards me, the big form of Henshaw."

"You had no idea who the lady was?" Edith Morriston interrupted him to ask.

"Naturally not the vaguest," Gifford answered. "When I had gone as far as was safe, I set myself to listen again.

"'I don't know what your game is or whether you think you can play the fool with me,' Henshaw was saying in an ugly tone. 'But I warn you not to try it; I am not a man to be fooled. Now let us be friends again,' he added in a softer tone.

"It seemed as though he put out his hand for a caress, for the girl started back and I heard her say 'Never!'

"'Folly!' he exclaimed. Then took a step forward. 'You are in love with another man?' he demanded. I could hear the hiss of the question.

"'If I were I should not tell you,' was the defiant reply in a low voice.

"'You would not?' he snapped viciously. 'Let me tell you this, then. You shall never marry another man while I live. I hold the bar to that, as you will find.'

"'You mean to act like a cad?' I heard the girl say.

"'I mean to act,' he retorted, 'like a sensible man who has a fair advantage and means, in spite of your caprice, to keep it.'

"'Fair?' the girl echoed in scorn.

"'Yes, fair,' Henshaw insisted with some heat. 'I saved you from a scandal that would have ruined you, and it was natural I should ask my reward. But your notions of gratitude, which had led me on to love you, soon evaporated; but I am not so easily dismissed.'

"'You mean to continue your cowardly persecution?' There was a tremor in the girl's voice that made me long to get at the man.

"'I mean to marry you,' he retorted. 'Or at least—'

"'Don't touch me!' she said hoarsely as he approached her.

"'You are coming away with me to-night,' he insisted. 'You need not pretend to be horrified. It won't be your first nocturnal adventure, and I have waited quite long enough.'

"He had driven her to the other corner on the window side of the room. As I leaned forward ready to fasten on the man when he should offer violence I heard a peculiar sound as of a loose piece of wood or iron striking the sill.

"'Keep away!' the girl said in a hoarse whisper. 'If you drive me to desperation I swear I will kill you.'

"There followed a vicious laugh from Henshaw and I could tell from the panting which followed that a struggle was going on. Just then the moon came out and I could see that Henshaw was trying to get some object—a weapon, I guessed—away from the girl. It is a wonder that neither of them saw me. In the dark opening I must have still been practically hidden, and they too intent on their struggle to notice anything beyond.

"I was just on the point of springing out to the girl's assistance when she staggered back and, turning, made a rush for the door. In a moment Henshaw was after her, but in his blind haste he either tripped or stumbled and fell heavily. I think it likely that in the dark he struck against the corner of the rather massive oak table in the centre of the room and was thrown off his balance. He rose immediately, but I was now close behind him, and as he put out his arm to clutch the girl, who was then half through the doorway, I gripped him by the collar and with all my strength swung him back into the room.

"He must have been most horribly surprised, for he uttered a gasping cry as he spun round, and instead of keeping his feet and rushing at me as I expected he went down with a thud by the window."

They had stopped in their walk now, and Edith Morriston was listening almost breathlessly to Gifford's graphic story. Never for a moment had he suggested the lady's identity; for all that had passed neither of them might have known it.

"I turned quickly to the door," Gifford continued, "but to my surprise the lady whom I expected to find there had disappeared. I could neither see nor hear any sign of her.

"I took a step back into the room, fully expecting an onslaught from the infuriated Henshaw. 'You cowardly brute!' I exclaimed in the heat of my anger and excitement. But no reply came, and to my wonder he lay still on the floor where he had fallen."

22
How Gifford Escaped

"I waited for some time in silence, expecting him every moment to rise and retaliate. He was a big, muscular man, but it never occurred to me to be in any fear of him physically. For one thing my indignation was too hot to admit fear; I happen to be quite good enough at boxing to be able to take care of myself, and I was sure— all the more from his continuing to lie there—that such a despicable bully must be a coward.

"'You had better get up and clear out of this house,' I said wrathfully, 'before you get the thrashing you so richly deserve.'

"No answer came. As I waited for one there was, save for my own breathing, dead silence in the room. Before speaking I had heard something like a long drawn sigh come from the man on the floor, but now, listening intently, I could hear nothing. Two explanations suggested themselves to account for his still lying there. One, shame at his vile conduct having been witnessed by a third person, the other that he had struck his head against the wall in falling and was stunned.

"Naturally I was not greatly concerned at the fellow's condition, whichever it was; still it would, I concluded, be well to settle the matter, and if he was merely skulking see that he cleared out of the house. I shut the door, and then crossing to where the man lay, struck a match and held it out to get a view of him.

"He lay on his face with his arms bent under him. I prodded him with my foot, but he did not stir; he lay absolutely, rather uncannily still. The match burned out; I struck another and leaned over to get a sight of his face.

To my horror there met my eyes a dark wet patch on the floor which I instinctively felt must be blood. You may imagine the terrible thrill the conviction gave me. Yet I could not believe even then that anything really serious had happened.

"I struck a fresh match and holding it up with one hand, with the other took the man's shoulder and turned him over on his back. Then I knew that I was there with a dead man. The hue of the face was unmistakably that of death. And the cause of it was plainly to be seen. There was a wound in the man's neck from which blood came freely.

"How had the wound—clearly a fatal one—been caused? I searched for an explanation. That which forced itself upon me was that the girl had in her desperation stabbed her persecutor with some weapon she had found there or brought with her. It was a horrible idea to entertain, although the act would have been almost justified. I wondered if by chance the weapon was still there. Striking a match I looked round. Yes; there on the floor near the spot where Henshaw had first fallen, lay a narrow blood-stained chisel.

"Whatever my first conclusions were I can see now the most probable explanation of how Henshaw came by his death-wound. He had forced the chisel away from the girl; he had kept it in his hand; in his eagerness to prevent his victim's escape he had not realized that he was holding it point upwards, and when he fell it had pierced him with all the force of his heavy body falling plump on it."

"Then you know it was an accident?" Edith Morriston drew a great breath of relief from the painful tension with which she had listened.

"I can see it was a pure accident," Gifford answered. "All the same it was an accident with an ugly look about it, and I quickly realized that I was in an equivocal—not to say dangerous, situation."

"It was a terrible predicament for you," the girl said sympathetically.

"It was indeed. And one which called for prompt action. Moreover the very fact that I was not in evening clothes made it all the more suspicious. I pulled my wits together and proceeded to make quite sure that the man was actually dead. That I found was beyond all doubt the case, and it now remained for me to make my escape before being found there in that hideous situation.

"I went out to the landing, closing the door after me, with the idea of getting down the stairs and escaping into the garden as secretly as I had come in. I had crept down a very few stairs when I found this was not to be. A chatter of voices just below told me that people were in the tower, and leaning over I could see couples passing between the passage to the hall and the room below me.

"At any moment, I realized, some of them might take it into their heads to explore the topmost room, when the result would be disastrous. Certainly in my mufti I could not get past the next floor just then without exciting fatal notice, and to wait for an opportunity when the coast might be clear was too dangerous, seeing the risk of someone coming up.

"It was not easy to see my way of escape. I went to the top room and locked the door. My nerves were pretty strong, but they were severely tried when I shut myself in with the dead man and had the consciousness of having laid myself open to the charge of being his murderer. I stood there by the door thinking desperately what I could do. Fool that I had been to venture into the place in that garb. But who could have foreseen the result? Anyhow there was no time for reflection; it was necessary to act and seek a possible expedient. Hopelessly enough I went into the little inner room and struck a match. In a moment a thrill of hope came to me, for the first object the light showed me was a big coil of rope conspicuous among the odds and ends of lumber in the recess. The idea of escape by the window had only occurred to me to be dismissed as a sheer impossibility; the height of the tower made that quite prohibitive, but here seemed a chance of it. If only the rope was long enough.

"I got hold of the coil as my match burned out, and pulled it away from the surrounding rubbish. Its weight gave me hope that it would be sufficient. In haste I dragged it to the outer room into which the moonlight was now streaming. With a shuddering glance at the dead man, whose ashen face stared up in ghastly fashion in the moonbeams, I opened the window and looked out to make sure that no one was below. Satisfied on that point I brought forward the rope and began paying it out of the window. To my content I saw that there was a strong iron stanchion at the side which would allow of the rope being fastened to it.

"There was light enough just then to enable me to see pretty well when the end of the rope reached the ground, and upon examining what was left in the room I calculated that not much more than half was outside. In a flash the discovery gave me an idea. Why should I not simply pass the rope behind the stanchion and use it doubled? By that means I could pull it down after me when I reached the ground, and so not only effect my escape but also leave the fact unknown. That, together with the door locked on the inside, would tend to make Henshaw's death a mystery with a strong probability in favour of suicide, which would be altogether the happiest conclusion to arrive at. In fact my hastily formed calculation was, as we know, subsequently borne out and the suicide theory would probably have been quietly accepted had it not been for the intervention of Gervase Henshaw with his smartness and incredulity.

"That is practically the end of my story, Miss Morriston. I laid the chisel by the body, went to the window, pulled in the rope, carefully got the centre, adjusted it through the stanchion, and with a last look at the dead man, got out of the window, a rather nerve-trying business, and began to lower myself. I had calculated that the double rope was long enough to take me to within a few feet of the ground, and this proved to be the case. When I came to the end I let go of one side and pulled the other with me as I dropped. Then I drew the rope down, the latter half when released falling with a great thud. Hastily I set off for the lake, dragging the rope after me. At the landing-stage by the boat-house I coiled it up as best I could and threw it in. As I had anticipated it was thick and heavy enough to sink without being weighted. Then with a last glance at the tower I made my way as quickly as possible to the hotel in a state of nerves which you may imagine, little thinking that my descent from the tower had been witnessed. My first intention was to abandon all idea of going to the dance, but on reflection I came to the conclusion that I had better at least put in an appearance there.

"Accordingly I changed and came on late to the ball, as you know. Naturally a great curiosity possessed me to find out the girl who had played the third part in the drama which had been enacted in the tower. But I had not seen her face, nor heard her voice sufficiently to be able to recognize it. There were several tall girls in the room, yourself among the number, but naturally it never occurred to me—"

He stopped awkwardly, just as by inadvertence he was about to say that which all along he had studiously refrained from suggesting.

"To suspect me," Edith Morriston completed his sentence with a smile.

"No," he continued frankly. "You would have been the last person to enter my head in that connection. And then Kelson came out of the passage from the tower with Miss Tredworth, to whom he had just proposed. He introduced me in a way which suggested their new relationship, and we had just began to chat when to my horror I noticed what to my mind went to prove that she was the person for whom I was looking. There were dark red stains on the white roses she wore on her dress. It was an unpleasant shock to me, placing me, as it seemed, in a terribly difficult position. For, at the first blush of my discovery, it all seemed to fit in. Clement Henshaw had been, I imagined, in love with Miss Tredworth before Kelson appeared on the scene. She had thrown him over for my friend, and Henshaw, taking his rejection in bad part, had threatened to expose some questionable incident in her past. Now that is all happily explained away, and I won't retrace the steps by which my imagination led me on; but you see how painfully I was situated with respect to my friend.

"That is my story, Miss Morriston. Had I known what I know now I should not have kept it to myself so long; but up to a certain point, until the last few days, there seemed no reason for making the dangerous secret known to anyone. Now, when it appears necessary to protect you from this man, Henshaw, the account of the part I played in the tragedy must be told in your interest."

Edith Morriston drew in a deep breath as Gifford ceased speaking. "It is very kind and chivalrous of you, Mr. Gifford," she said in a low voice, "to run this risk for me, although your telling me the story shall never involve you in danger."

"I am ready for your sake to face any danger the telling of my secret may hold for me," he responded firmly.

"I am sure of that, as I am sure of you," she replied. Then added with a change of tone, "You were certain for a while that Muriel Tredworth had not only been guilty of something discreditable in her past but had stabbed to death in your presence the man who knew her secret."

"I'm afraid there seemed to me no alternative but to believe it," he acknowledged.

"When you found out that you were mistaken in her identity and that she had nothing whatever to do with the tragedy you would naturally transfer the opinion you had held of her to—to the other woman—the one who was actually there?"

The question was put searchingly and was not to be evaded.

"That would be a natural consequence," Gifford admitted frankly. "But there was in my mind always a growing doubt whether the wound had not been given accidentally. And that doubt became almost certainty when the real identity of Henshaw's victim became apparent."

Edith Morriston looked at him steadily. "You know it—for certain?" she asked almost coldly.

"Naturally I cannot fail to know it now," he answered sympathetically.

She gave a rather bitter laugh. "I shall not deny it to you, Mr. Gifford, even if I thought it could be of any use. But, knowing so much, you owe it to me to hear my explanation of matters which look so black against me, and above all to accept my absolute assurance that so far as I am concerned Clement Henshaw's wound was quite accidental. Indeed I never dreamt that he had been hurt until his body was found."

Gifford seized her hand by an irresistible impulse.

"Miss Morriston, if you only knew how glad and relieved I am to hear you say that!" he exclaimed.

"When you hear my story," she said, composedly but with an underlying bitterness which was hardly to be concealed, "the story of a long martyrdom of persecution—for it has been nothing less—you will acquit me of being guilty of anything disreputable. What I did was innocent enough and it moreover was forced upon me."

"Tell me," he urged tenderly.

"I must tell you," she returned, "if only to set myself right in your eyes who have been witness of the terrible sequel to it all. But not to-night; it is too late, and the story is long: it must be told at length. Dick will be home by this and I must go. I would ask you to come in, but there would be no opportunity for private talk there. Will you meet me to-morrow morning at half-past ten by the summer-house near the wood that runs up to James' farm? You know it?"

"Well. I will be there."

"It is rather a long way for you to come," she said, "but there are reasons for avoiding the big wood with the rides."

"I know," he replied. "Henshaw might be on the look-out there for you." Then he added in answer to her quick look of curiosity, "I happened once by accident to see him there with you."

"Ah, yes," she admitted with a shudder, "I will tell you about that."

"I think I can guess," he said quietly. "Now in the meantime you will take no notice of this man if he writes or tries to see you. He will probably be exasperated by your not keeping the appointment this evening and may determine to put the screw on."

"Yes," she agreed with a lingering fear in her voice.

"Leave him to me to deal with," Gifford said reassuringly. "And do make up your mind that all will be well."

"I will, thanks to you, my friend in need."

And so, with a warm pressure of the hands, they parted.

23
EDITH MORRISTON'S STORY

Next morning Gifford was in good time at the rendezvous, a sequestered corner of the park, and Edith Morriston soon joined him. "Let us come into the summer-house," she suggested; "it will be more convenient for my long story."

"First of all, tell me," Gifford said, "has anything happened since last night? Has Henshaw made any move?"

She took out a note and handed it to him. "Only that," she said with an uneasy laugh.

"There must have been some misunderstanding last evening," Gifford read. "I cannot think that your not keeping the appointment was intentional. Anyhow I can wait till to-night, then I shall be at the lane just beyond the church at 7.30. That you may not repent I hope you have not repented." That was all.

"A thinly veiled threat," Gifford observed. "The man in his way seems as great a bully as his brother. May I keep this? I am going to see Mr. Henshaw presently, and have a serious talk with him. After which I shall hope to be able to convince you that your troubles are at an end."

"If you can do that—" she said.

"The knowledge that I have been of service to you will be my great reward. I hope I am sufficiently a gentleman not to ask or expect any other."

She made no reply. They had entered the little rustic summer-house, and sat down.

"Dick has driven into Branchester," Edith Morriston said, perhaps to end an embarrassing pause. "He will not be back till luncheon, so we are not likely to be interrupted."

"That's well," Gifford answered. "Now please begin what I am most anxious to hear."

"The story I have to tell you, Mr. Gifford," Edith Morriston began, "is not a pleasant one and is as humiliating to me to relate as was the experience, the terrible experience, I had to go through. But to be fair to myself I must be quite frank with you, and am sure you will never give me cause to repent speaking unreservedly."

"You can rely upon my honour to respect your confidence," Gifford responded warmly.

"I know I may," the girl answered. "Well, then, you must know first of all, that my father married a second time, and he unfortunately chose a woman well connected enough, but heartless and an utter snob. I suppose men are often blind to these hateful qualities before marriage; doubtless a clever, unscrupulous woman is able to hide her faults when she has the main chance in view. My stepmother was a good deal younger than my father, and I dare say on the whole made him, socially at any rate, a fairly good wife. Her one idea was social aggrandizement at any cost, and I unhappily was to fall a victim to it.

"I suppose we ought not to blame her for determining that I ought to marry well; she wanted to do the best for the family and was constitutionally incapable of making allowance for or considering any one's private feelings. To make a long story short, my stepmother, in pursuance of her policy, determined that I should marry a certain peer whose name I need not mention. He was altogether a bad lot, and I soon came to know it. I received certain warnings, but without them I could see that the man was all wrong, and I told my stepmother what I thought of him.

"She scoffed at the idea that he was any worse than the average man. All I had to concern myself with was the fact that he was a peer of ancient lineage, of large property, and there wasn't another girl in the kingdom who wouldn't jump at him. I might well chance his making me unhappy since he could make me a countess, and to refuse him would be absolute madness; Mrs. Morriston's face grew black at the very thought of it. She soon got my father on to her side, and between them I had a hateful time of it. It's the old story, which will be told as long as there are worldly, selfish women on the earth, but it was none the less fresh and poignant to me who had to live through the experience.

"Things got so bad through my continued refusal to fall in with my stepmother's wishes that I was reduced to a state bordering on despair. My father, whom I loved, was turned against me; his mind was so prejudiced in favour of the man whom I was being gradually forced to take as a husband that he could see no good reason, only sheer obstinacy, in my refusal. Altogether my life was becoming a perfect hell. Dick, who might have stood by me, and made things less unbearable, was away on a two years' tour for big game shooting; I had no one to confide in, no one to help me.

"Just as things were at their worst and I was getting quite desperate, I met at a dance a man named Archie Jolliffe. He had been a sailor, but having come into money had given up the Service and settled down to enjoy himself. He and I got on very well together from the first; he was a breezy, genial, young fellow, fond of fun and adventure and a pleasant contrast in every way to the man who was threatening to ruin my life. I don't know that in happier circumstances I should have cared for Jolliffe; there wasn't much in him beyond his capacity for fun; he was inclined to be fast in a foolish sort of way; a man's man rather than one for whom a woman could feel much respect. Still he was not vicious like the other, for whom my dislike increased every time I saw him.

"Well, Archie Jolliffe fell in love with me and in his impetuous way made no secret of it. I need not say it did not take long for my step-mother to become aware of it, and with the idea that I was encouraging him she became furious. Except that poor Archie was a welcome change from the atmosphere of my home and the hateful attentions of the man who was always being left alone with me, I did not really care for him, and but for Mrs. Morriston's attitude I should have told him it was no use his thinking of me. Considering the sequel, I wish I had done so; but it is too late now for regrets. His love-making gave me a chance of defying my stepmother, and I rather enjoyed baulking her plans to keep Archie and me apart. If I did not encourage him—indeed, I refused him every time he proposed—I did not dismiss him as I ought to have done, and he evidently had an idea that perseverance would win the day. And so, after a fashion, it did.

"Matters reached such a pitch at last that it became plain that I must either consent to marry the man I loathed or leave my home for good. Goaded on by my apparent encouragement of Archie Jolliffe, my stepmother resolved to bring matters to a crisis. She started a terrific row with me one day, my father was brought into it, and I stood up against them both. The upshot was that when the interview was over I went out of the house boiling with indignation and for the time utterly reckless. Chance caught the psychological moment and threw me in the way of Archie Jolliffe. He saw something was wrong and pressed me to tell him what had happened. He was so chivalrous and sympathetic that I was led in my turbulent state of mind to become confidential, the more so when he told me he had known for some time how I was being treated.

"'You must not marry that man,' he said 'It is an outrage for your people to suggest such a thing. He is a big swell and all that, with heaps of money, but any man in town who knows anything will tell you he is quite impossible,'

"I had heard that, and had told my stepmother, but of course it did not suit her to heed me. She cared for nothing beyond the fact that I should be a countess, and said so.

"Archie and I talked together for a long time and with the result that in my longing for protection from the powers against me and my indignation at the way I was being treated I had promised when we parted to marry him, and we had planned to elope together that very night.

"At that time we were living at Haynthorpe Hall–you know it?–about ten miles from here. That evening I slipped out of the house after dinner and met Archie, who was waiting for me at a quiet spot outside the village. His plan was to drive across country to Branchester Junction, where it was not likely we should be noticed or recognized, catch the night train up to town and be married there next morning. You may imagine the state of desperation–utter desperation and recklessness–I was in to have consented to such a thing, but I could see no help for it, and of two evils I seemed to be choosing the least. The future looked hideously vague and dark; still Jolliffe was capable of being transformed into a decent husband, while the other man assuredly was not.

"Archie seemed overjoyed, poor fellow, as I mounted into the dog-cart; he had hardly expected that I should not repent. Once we were fairly off and bowling along the dark road, a sense of relief came to me, and whatever qualms I may have felt soon vanished. However wrong my conduct was I had been driven to it and my father, for whom I was sorry, by taking part against me, deserved to lose me.

"My companion had the tact not to talk much, and I was glad to think he could realize the seriousness of the step he had persuaded me to take. But the little he did say was affectionately sympathetic and, now that the die was cast, it comforted me to indulge hopes of him.

"All went well till we were about three miles from Branchester; then an awful thing happened. Our horse was a fast trotter, and Archie let him have his head, knowing that it would never do for us to miss the train. As we turned a blind corner we came into collision with another dog-cart which we had neither seen nor heard. The force of the impact was so great that our off-wheel was smashed; the cart went over, we were both flung out, and as I fell I realized horribly that my desperate expedient was a failure.

"I was not much hurt, for my fall was broken, and I soon scrambled to my feet. But Archie lay there motionless. The man who was the only occupant of the other dog-cart had pulled into the hedge and alighted. He came up to offer his help, and to express his sorrow at the accident, which he said, doubtless with truth, was not his fault. I dare say you will have guessed that the man was Clement Henshaw. Between us we raised Archie and carried him to the side of the road. He was quite insensible, and breathing heavily.

"'I am afraid he is rather seriously hurt,' the man said sympathetically. 'We ought to get him to Branchester Hospital as soon as possible.'

"I was so overwhelmed by the sudden and terrible end to our adventure that I could think of nothing. By a great piece of luck a belated dray came along on its way to Branchester. Into this, with the driver's help, we lifted poor Archie; and then Henshaw and I drove on in his trap to prepare the hospital authorities for the patient's arrival. The doctor after a cursory examination gave very little hope, and I left the hospital in a most wretched state of mind, feeling more than indirectly responsible for the end of that bright young life. Henshaw arranged for the horse and smashed dogcart to be fetched from the scene of the accident, and then he asked where in the town he should escort me.

"I thanked him and said, a good deal to his surprise, that I was not going to stop in Branchester, but would hire a fly and drive to my destination. I stood, of course, in a hideously false position, and that he very soon began to divine; he would not hear of my getting a fly at that hour of the night, but insisted on driving me in his trap to wherever I wished to go.

"Unhappily I had no idea of the man's character, or I should never have dreamt of accepting his offer; but I was then in no state of mind to judge his nature or question his motives; he had proved himself infinitely kind and resourceful, so in my lonely and agitated condition I consented, little imagining what the dire result to me would be.

"On the drive back to my home I was naturally in a horribly distressed state of mind, and hardly dared think of the future. My companion tactfully refrained from much talking, although I had an idea that his curiosity was greatly excited to learn the explanation of the affair; he put occasionally a leading question which I always evaded, when he took the hint and did not press his inquiries. So far as every one else was concerned there had been no idea of connecting me with poor Archie Jolliffe. The hospital people believed that he had been driving alone, and that I had been in the trap with Henshaw. I dare say they took me for his sister or his wife.

"At last, after one of the most wretched hours I ever spent—and I have had more than my fair share of trouble— we reached Haynthorpe, and on the outskirts of the village I asked Henshaw to set me down. He stopped and looked at me curiously.

"'Can't you trust me to drive you to your home?'" he said insinuatingly.

"I replied that I preferred to get down where we were, and thanked him as warmly as I was able for all his services.

"'You haven't even told me your name,' he protested, 'Mine is Clement Henshaw; I am staying at Flinton for hunting.'

"My answer was that he must not think me ungrateful, but that I would rather not tell him my name. It could be of no consequence to him.

"'I should like at least,' he urged, 'to be allowed to drive over and report how your–friend–or was it your brother?–is getting on.'

"I thanked him, made the best excuse I could for refusing, got down from the trap and hurried off through the dark village street, thankful to get away from those awkward questions.

"But if I thought I had finally got rid of Mr. Clement Henshaw I was, in my ignorance of the man, woefully mistaken."

24
HOW THE STORY ENDED

"When I reached the house luck unexpectedly favoured me. My maid, whom I had been obliged to take, up to a certain point, into my confidence, and who, after the manner of her class, had acquired more than a sympathetic inkling of the way my people had been treating me, was waiting up on the look-out for my return, and quietly let me in. She told me that no one but herself had any idea that I was out of the house; she had led them to believe that I had gone to bed early with a headache, which considering the stress of the past two days was plausible enough. So I got back safely to my room which it had not seemed likely. I should ever enter again, and next morning I could see that my over-night's adventure was quite unsuspected.

"Naturally I anticipated a continuation of my stepmother's attempts to force me into the marriage she had in view, and it rather puzzled me to understand why they seemed to be dropped. The prospective bridegroom did not come to the house, and, stranger still, his name was not mentioned. The explanation was soon forthcoming. I did not see the newspapers just then, in fact I have an idea they were purposely kept away from me; but some people who were calling mentioned a big society-scandal coming on in the Law Courts in which this precious peer was desperately involved. The relief with which I heard the news was unbounded considering all it meant for me, but my joy was turned to bitter grief by the news that Archie Jolliffe after lying unconscious for nearly a week had died of his injury. I had contrived, during the days he lingered, to make secret inquiries as to his condition, and so knew that what would have seemed my heartless absence from his bedside had made no difference to him."

"Poor fellow," Gifford commented.

"It was unspeakably sad," Edith Morriston continued, "but it seemed like fate, seeing how things rearranged themselves afterwards. Certainly if I was to blame for his piteous end, I was to pay the penalty. For no sooner was I out of one trouble than another was ready for me.

"After this long preface, I come to the most unpleasant episode of Henshaw and his persecution.

"On the day I heard of poor Archie's death I had gone out for a walk possessed by a great longing to be alone in my grief. On my way home by a woodland path leading to the Hall grounds, I, to my great annoyance, came upon Clement Henshaw. I can't say I was altogether surprised, for I had caught a glimpse of some one very like him in the village a day or two before. Of that I had thought little, merely taking care that the man did not see me. But now there was no avoiding him, and I had more than a suspicion that he had been lying in wait for me. At the risk of appearing horribly ungrateful I made up my mind on the instant to try to pass him with a bow, but need not say that was utterly futile. He stood directly in my path, and raised his hat.

"'I am sorry to be the bearer of sad news, Miss Morriston,' he said.

"So he had found out my name, assuredly not by accident, and the fact angered me, perhaps unreasonably.

"'I have heard of Mr. Jolliffe's death,' I replied coldly, 'if that is what you have to tell me.'

"'I thought,' he rejoined, with assurance, 'it quite possible you might not have heard so soon.'

"From his manner I began to see that the man was likely to become an annoyance if he were not snubbed, but soon discovered that it was not so easily done. I thanked him coldly enough, and tried to dismiss him, but he insisted on walking with me. What could I do? He seemed determined to force his company upon me and I could not run away. He tried to get out of me how I had come to be driving with Archie that night, and although I evaded his questions it was plain that he had a shrewd inkling of the reason. Not to weary you with a long account of this disagreeable and humiliating affair, I will only say that from that day forward I became subject to a determined system of persecution from Clement Henshaw. He waylaid me on every possible occasion, holding over me a covert threat of the exposure of my escapade, till at last I was absolutely afraid to go outside the house for fear of meeting him."

"He wanted to marry you?" Gifford suggested.

Edith Morriston gave a little shudder. "I suppose so. He was always making love to me, and was quite impervious to snubbing. When, in consequence of my keeping within bounds of the house and garden, he could not see me, he took to writing, and kept me in terror lest one of his letters should fall into my stepmother's hands. I wished afterwards that I had taken a bold line, confessed what had happened, and defied the consequences. I think it was the fear of being disgraced in my brother's eyes on his return which kept me from doing so.

"In the midst of my worry my father fell into a state of bad health and we took him down to the Devonshire coast for change of air. Needless to say Henshaw soon found out our retreat, and to my dismay appeared there. His persecution went on with renewed vigour and I, having less chance there of escaping it, was nearly at my wits' end, when fate curiously enough again intervened. We were caught in a storm on a long country excursion, my stepmother got a severe chill and within a week was dead. We returned to Haynthorpe, my father being now in a very precarious state of health, Henshaw followed us with a pertinacity that was almost devilish. But I now ventured to defy his threats of exposing me; he strenuously denied any such intention and declared himself madly in love with me. I had now taken courage enough to reject him uncompromisingly; I forbade him ever to speak to me again, and, as after that he disappeared from the village, began to flatter myself that I had got rid of him.

"My father grew worse now from day to day; he lingered through the summer and with the chill days of autumn the end came. Dick hurried home and arrived just in time to see him alive. He left a much larger fortune than we had supposed him to possess, and Dick, always fond of sport, was soon in negotiation for this place which had come into the market.

"No sooner had we settled in here than, to my horror, Clement Henshaw began to renew his persecution. He had evidently heard that I had inherited a good share of my father's fortune, and was worth making another effort for. He recommenced to write to me, he came down secretly and waylaid me, and when everything else failed he resorted to threats, not veiled as before, but open and unmistakable. He vowed that if I persisted in refusing to marry him he would take good care that I should never marry anyone else. He held, he said, my reputation in his hand; he hoped he should never have to use his power, but I ought to consider the state of his feelings towards me and not goad him to desperate measures. In short he took all the joy out of my life, for I had come from mere dislike simply to loathe the man who could show himself such a dastardly cad. And the worst of it was that I saw no way out of it. Dick is a good fellow and very fond of me, but, although you might not think it, he is almost absurdly proud of the family name and its unsmirched record. And if I had confided in him, and he had horsewhipped Henshaw, what good could that have done? It would simply have infuriated the man, who would have at once made public my escapade, and few people would have given me the credit of its being innocent. Dick had just sunk a large part of his fortune in this place, he had taken over the hounds and was certain of becoming popular. All that would be nullified and upset if this man, Henshaw, chose to let loose his tongue. For how could I even pretend to deny his story? At the very least the truth would mean a hateful reflection on my dead father, and the whole thing would have led to an intolerable scandal. Yet it seemed as though this could be avoided in no other way but by marrying my persecutor, a man whom I had reason to hate and who had shown himself to be such an unchivalrous bully. About this time—that is shortly before the Hunt Ball—rumours had got about the neighbourhood that I was going to marry Lord Painswick. He was certainly paying me a good deal of attention, and I fancy Dick would have liked the match, but I could not bring myself to care for Painswick, and indeed his courtship only added to my other worries.

"But Clement Henshaw heard the rumour and it had naturally the effect of rousing his wretched pursuit of me to greater activity. He vowed with brutal vehemence that I should not marry Painswick, and declared that when our engagement was announced he would tell him the story he had against me. That in itself did not trouble me much since I had no intention of marrying Painswick; still the man's relentless persecution was getting more than I could bear.

"I now come to the night of the Hunt Ball. For some days previously I had seen or heard nothing of Henshaw, and had even begun to hope that something might have happened to make the man abandon his line of conduct. I might have known him better. To my intense annoyance and dismay I saw him come into the ballroom with all the hateful assurance that was so familiar to me. I could not well escape, seeing that I was acting as hostess. For a while he, beyond a formal greeting, let me alone. But I felt what was surely coming, and it was almost a relief when he took an opportunity of asking for a dance.

"He must have seen the hate in my eyes as in my hesitation they met his, for he said with a forced laugh, 'You need not do violence to your feelings by dancing with me, Miss Morriston, if you don't care to, but there is something I must say to you. Let us come out of the crowd to where we shall not be overheard.'

"I had never felt so madly furious with the man as at that moment; and it was with a reckless desire to tell him in strong language my opinion of his tactics, to insult him, if that were possible, to declare that I would die rather than yield to him, that I led the way to the tower. My desire to get out of the crowd was even greater than his, for a mad hope possessed me that in some desperate way I might bring our relations to a final issue.

"We went into the sitting-out room. 'Some one will be coming in here,' he objected. 'Is there a room upstairs where we can talk?'

"'There is a room up there,' I answered, as steadily as my indignation would let me, and unheeding the idea of compromising myself I went up the dark staircase in front of him. Naturally the idea that our stormy interview was to have a witness would have been the last thing to enter my mind; it never occurred to me to make sure no one was already in the room when we entered it.

"You know what happened, Mr. Gifford, so I need not go through that. The man showed himself the cowardly bully that he was. Somehow up there alone with him, as at least I thought, in the dark, my courage gave way, and it was only when the man sought in his vehemence to take hold of me that anger and disgust cast out fear. It was quite by accident that I touched and caught up the chisel lying on the window-sill. As the man's hand sought me it struck the edge of the chisel, and got a wound; that must have been how the blood came upon my dress. He seized my arm, and after a struggle wrenched the implement away. But I never struck him with it, far from giving him his death-blow. The chisel was never in my hand afterwards. When I rushed for the door in a sudden panic, for, knowing that I had hurt him, I believed the man in his rage might be capable of anything, and when in springing after me he stumbled and fell, the chisel must have been held by him edge upwards, and so pierced him to his death."

"That, I am certain now," Gifford said, "is what must have happened."

"And you thought I had stabbed him?" the girl said with a reproachful smile.

"I hardly dare ask you to forgive me for harbouring such a thought," he replied. "Yet had it been true I, who had been a witness of the man's vile conduct, could never have blamed you. If ever an act was justifiable—"

An elongated shadow shot forward on the ground in front of them. Gifford stopped abruptly, and with an involuntary action his companion clutched his arm as both looked up expectantly. Next moment Gervase Henshaw stood before them.

25
DEFIANCE

For some moments Henshaw did not speak; indeed, it was probable that the unexpected success of his search for Edith Morriston—for such doubtless was his object—had so disagreeably startled him, that he was unable to pull those sharp wits of his together at once. But the expression which flashed into his eyes, and that came instantaneously, was of so vengeful and threatening a character, that Gifford felt glad he was there to protect the girl from her now enraged persecutor.

"I did not expect to find you here, Miss Morriston."

The words came sharply and wrathfully, when the man had found his glib tongue.

Gifford answered. "Miss Morriston and I have been enjoying the view and the air of the pines."

The commonplace remark naturally, as it was intended, went for nothing. Henshaw affected not to notice it.

"I am glad I have come across you, Miss Morriston," he said, with an evident curbing of his chagrin, "as I have something rather important to say to you."

"I am afraid I cannot hear it now, Mr. Henshaw," the girl returned coldly.

Henshaw's face darkened. "I really must ask you to grant me an interview without delay," he retorted insistently, as though secure in his sense of power over the girl. "I am sure Mr. Gifford will permit—"

"Mr. Gifford will do nothing of the sort," came the bold and rather startling reply from the person alluded to. "As a friend of Miss Morriston's I do not intend to allow you to hold any more private conversations with her."

No doubt with his knowledge of the world and of his own advantage Henshaw put down Gifford's resolute speech to mere bluff. And Gervase Henshaw was too old a legal practitioner to be bluffed. "I do not for a moment admit your right to interfere," he retorted with an assumption of calm superiority. "I am addressing myself to Miss Morriston, who does not, I hope, approve of your somewhat singular manners."

Gifford took a step out of the summerhouse and sternly faced Henshaw. "I am sure Miss Morriston will endorse anything I choose to say to a man who has constituted himself her cowardly persecutor," he said. "Now we don't want to have a dispute in a lady's presence," he added as Henshaw began an angry rejoinder. "You have got, unless you wish very unpleasant consequences to follow, to render an account to me, as Miss Morriston's friend, of your abominable conduct towards her. But not here. You had better come to my room at the hotel at three o'clock this afternoon and hear what I shall have to say. And in the meantime you will address Miss Morriston only at the risk of a horsewhipping."

Henshaw was looking at him steadfastly through eyes that blazed with hate. "I wonder if you quite know whom and what you are trying to champion," he snarled.

"Perfectly," was the cool reply. "A much wronged and cruelly persecuted lady. You had better postpone what you have to say till this afternoon, when we will come to an understanding as to your conduct. Now, as you are on private land, you had better take the nearest way to the public road."

Henshaw looked as though he would have liked to bring the dispute to the issue of a physical encounter, had but the coward in him dared. "I am here by permission," he returned, standing his ground.

"Which has been rescinded by the vile use to which you have chosen to put it," Gifford rejoined. "I have Miss

Morriston's authority to treat you as a trespasser, and to order you off her brother's land."

Henshaw fell back a step. "Very well, Mr. Gifford," he returned with an ugly sneer. "You talk with great confidence now, but we shall see. You will be wiser by this time tomorrow."

With that he turned and walked off; Gifford, after watching him for a while, went back to the summer-house.

"I have put things in the right train there," he remarked with a confident laugh. "I hope to be able to tell you this evening that Mr. Henshaw is a thing of the past."

"You are very sanguine," she said, a little doubtfully. "I am afraid you do not know the man."

"I'm afraid I do," he replied. "He is obviously not an easy person to deal with. But I think I see my way. Tell me. He has threatened you in order to induce you to elope with him?"

"Yes. He has found evidence among his brother's correspondence of the hold he had over me and of his persecution. That would afford a sufficient motive for my killing him; and how could I prove that I did not strike the blow?"

"It might be difficult," Gifford answered thoughtfully. "But I may be able to do it. Of course he knows you to be an heiress."

"I am sure of that from something he once let slip. It has been my inheritance which has brought all this trouble upon me, at any rate its persistency."

"Yes. This man must be something of an adventurer, as his brother was. We shall see," Gifford said with a grim touch. "Now, I must not keep you any longer. I am so grateful for the confidence you have given me. May I call later on and tell you the result?"

Her eyes were on him in an almost piteous searching for hope in his resolute face. "Of course," she responded. "I shall be so terribly anxious to know."

Chivalrously avoiding any suggestion of tenderness, he shook hands and went off towards the town.

26
Issue Joined

Punctually at the appointed time Gervase Henshaw was shown into Gifford's room. Kelson had received from his friend a hint of what was afoot and had naturally offered his services to back Gifford up, but they were refused.

"It is very kind of you, Harry," Gifford had said, "and just what one would have expected from you. But, as you shall hear later, this is not a business in which you or anyone could usefully intervene. In fact it would be dangerous for me, considering the man I am dealing with, to say what I have to say before a third person."

So Kelson went off to spend the afternoon at the Tredworths'.

When Henshaw came in his expression bore no indication of the terms on which he and Gifford had lately parted. The keen face was unruffled and almost genial; but Gifford was not the man to be deceived by that outward seeming. Henshaw bowed and took the chair the other indicated. There was a short pause as though each waited for the other to begin. In the end it was Gifford who spoke first.

"I should like to come to an understanding with you, Mr. Henshaw, with regard to a very serious annoyance, not to say persecution, to which Miss Morriston has been subjected at your hands." Henshaw drew back his thin lips in a smile. "I have to tell you," Gifford continued, "once and for all that it must cease."

"Miss Morriston authorizes you to tell me that?" The question was put with something like a sneer.

"I should hope it requires no authority," Gifford retorted. "Having cognizance of what has been going on, it is my plain duty–"

"Why yours?" Henshaw interrupted coolly.

"For a very good reason," Gifford replied; "one which I may have to tell you presently."

He saw Henshaw flush and dart a glance of hate at him. It was plain he had misinterpreted the reply. But the exhibition was only momentary.

"Admitting in the meantime your right to interfere," Henshaw said, now with perfect coolness, "allow me to tell you that you are taking a very foolish course."

"I shall be glad to know how."

"The reason is, that if you have any regard, as you suggest, for Miss Morriston, you are going the right way to do her a terrible injury."

Gifford rose and stood by the fire-place. "To come to the point at once without further preliminary fencing," he said quietly, "you mean, I take it, that I am forcing you to denounce her as being guilty of your brother's death."

For an instant Henshaw seemed taken aback by the other's directness. "There can be no doubt, holding the evidence I do, that she was guilty of it," he retorted uncompromisingly.

"I beg your pardon, Mr. Henshaw," Gifford objected with decision, "there can be, and is, a very great deal more than a doubt of it."

Henshaw shot a searching glance at the man who spoke so confidently, as though trying to probe what, if anything, was behind his words.

"Perhaps you know then," he returned with his sneering smile, "how otherwise, if the lady had no hand in it, my brother came by his death?"

"I do," was the quiet answer.

"Then," still the smile of sneering incredulity, "it is clearly your duty to make it known."

"Clearly," Gifford assented in a calm tone. "That is why I asked you to come here this afternoon."

Henshaw was looking at him with a sort of malicious curiosity. In spite of his smartness he seemed at a loss to divine what the other was driving at, unless it were a well-studied line of bluff. But that Gifford could have, apart from what Edith Morriston might have told him, any intimate knowledge of the tragedy was inconceivable.

"I shall be glad to hear what you have to say, Mr. Gifford," he responded, in perhaps much greater curiosity than he chose to show.

"Then I have to inform you positively," Gifford answered, "that your brother's fatal wound was the result of a pure accident."

Coming from Edith Morriston's champion, there was nothing surprising in that assertion. Certainly if that were the other's strong suit he could easily beat it. It was therefore in a tone of confidence and relief that he demanded, "You can prove it?"

"I can."

"By Miss Morriston's testimony?"

"Not at all. By my own."

"Your own?" Henshaw's question was put with a curling lip.

"My own," Gifford repeated steadfastly.

"May one ask what you mean by that?"

Henshaw's contemptuous incredulity was by no means diminished even by the other's confident attitude.

Gifford gave a short laugh. "Naturally you do not take my meaning. Obviously you think I am not a competent witness, that I know nothing except by hearsay. You are, extraordinary as it may seem, quite wrong. My testimony would be of nothing but what I myself saw and heard."

"What do you mean?" Henshaw had for a moment seemed to be calculating the probability of this monstrous suggestion being a fact, and had dismissed it with the contempt which showed itself in his question.

"I mean," Gifford replied with quiet assurance, "that I happened to be a witness of the interview in the tower-room between your brother and Miss Morriston, that I was there when he received his death-wound, and that it was I whom the girl Haynes saw descending by a rope from the top window."

Henshaw had started to his feet, his face working with an almost passionate astonishment. "You—you tell me all that," he cried, "and expect me to believe it?"

"I have told you and shall tell you nothing," was the cool reply, "that I am not prepared to state on oath in the witness-box."

For a while Henshaw seemed without the power to reply, dumbfounded, as his active brain tried to realize the probabilities of the declaration. "It seems to me," he said at length in a voice of which he was scarcely master, "that, whether your statement is true or otherwise, you are placing yourself in an uncommonly dangerous position, Mr. Gifford."

"I am aware that I am inviting a certain amount of ugly suspicion," Gifford agreed, "but the truth, which might have remained a mystery, has been forced from me by the necessity of protecting Miss Morriston. Perhaps you had better hear a frank account of the whole story, and the explanation of what I admit you are so far justified in setting down as concocted and wildly improbable."

"I should very much like to hear it," Henshaw returned in a tone which held out no promise of credence.

Thereupon Gifford gave him a terse account of the events and the chance which had led him into the tower and to be a secret witness of what happened there. Remembering that he was addressing the dead man's brother, he recounted the details of the interview without feeling; indeed he threw no more colour into it than if he had been opening a case in court. He simply stated the facts without comment. Henshaw listened to the singular story in an attitude of doggedly unemotional attention. Lawyer-like he restrained all tendency to interrupt the narrative and asked no question as it proceeded.

Nevertheless it was clear he was thinking keenly, eager to note any weak points which he could turn to use.

When the recital had come to an end he said coolly–

"Your story is a very extraordinary one, Mr. Gifford; I won't call it, as it seems at first sight, wildly improbable, but it is at any rate an almost incredible coincidence. With your knowledge of the law I need scarcely remind you that the facts as you have just recounted them place you in a rather unenviable position."

"As I have already said," Gifford replied, "my story is calculated to suggest suspicion against me. But I am prepared to risk that consequence."

"In court," Henshaw observed, with a malicious smile, "handled by a counsel who knew his business, your statement could be given a very ugly turn indeed."

"As I have just told you," Gifford returned quietly, "I would take that risk rather than allow Miss Morriston to remain longer under suspicion. As for myself I should have every confidence in the result."

"It is well to be sanguine," Henshaw sneered. "If you have not already done so, are you prepared to repeat your story to the police?"

"Most certainly I am, if necessary," was the prompt answer. "But I do not fancy you will wish me to do so."

Henshaw's look was one of surprise, real or affected. "Indeed? Why so?"

"I will tell you," Gifford replied with a touch of sternness. "Because it would be absolutely against your interest. For one thing it would, short of absolute proof, leave still the shadow of doubt over your brother's death, it would effectually put a stop to your designs on Miss Morriston, which in any case must come to an end, and it would show up your dead brother's character and conduct in a very disreputable light. Now what I have to say to you is this. I know that, following in your brother's footsteps, you have been subjecting Miss Morriston to an amount of very hateful persecution. There may have been a certain excuse for it, at any rate a degree of temptation, but your designs have not been welcome to the lady, and they must forthwith come to an end. Now unless you undertake to cease your attentions to Miss Morriston, in short to put an end at once and for all to this persecution, I shall effectually remove the hold you imagine you have over her by going straight to the police, giving them the real story of what happened in the tower that night and as a natural consequence shall give evidence to that effect at the adjourned inquest. You will know best whether it would be worth your while to force me to do this. I simply state the position."

He waited for Henshaw's answer. The man was plainly cornered and seemed to be divided between a desire to let Gifford go on and place himself in a dangerous situation, and the more expedient course of raising a scandal which would touch him as well as disgrace his dead brother.

"This is a clever piece of bluff, Mr. Gifford," he said at length; "but—"

"It is no bluff at all," Gifford interrupted firmly. "I am merely determined to take the obvious course to save Miss Morriston from something a good deal worse than annoyance. I have no wish to discredit the dead, but I must remind you that the persecution of Miss Morriston by your brother had gone on for a very considerable time, and had latterly developed into an atrocious system of bullying. It is not an occasion for mincing one's expressions, and I must say that in my opinion your own conduct has been very little, if any, better; and that will be the judgment of every decent man if the truth comes out, as come out it shall, unless you agree to my terms before you leave this room."

For a while Henshaw made no reply. He sat thinking strenuously, evidently weighing his chances, estimating the strength of his adversary's position. Now and again he shot a glance, half probing, half sullen, at Gifford, who leaned back against the mantelpiece coolly awaiting his answer. At length he spoke.

"This is a very fine piece of bravado, Mr. Gifford. But I am not such a fool as it pleases you to think me. It is very good of you to explain to me my position in this affair; I am, however, quite capable of seeing that for myself. And you can hardly expect me to look upon your gratuitous advice as disinterested."

The man was talking to gain time; Gifford shrewdly guessed that. "I might be pardoned for supposing you do not altogether realize how you stand," he replied quietly. "But, after all, that is, as you suggest, your affair."

Henshaw forced a smile. "The point of view is everything," he said in a preoccupied tone; "and ours, yours and mine, are diametrically opposed."

"The point of view which perhaps ought most to be considered," Gifford retorted with rising impatience, "is that of the honourable profession to which we both belong. If you are prepared to face the odium, professional and social, of an exposure—"

Henshaw interrupted him with a wave of the hand. "You may apply that to yourself and to your friend, Miss Morriston," he said sharply. "I can take care of myself, thank you."

Gifford shrugged. "Very well, then. There is no more to be said." He crossed the room and took up his hat. "I will go and see Major Freeman at once." At the door he turned, to see with surprise and a certain satisfaction that Henshaw, although he had risen from his chair, seemed in no hurry to move. "You are coming with me," he suggested. "It would be quite in order, I think, for you to be present at my statement—unless you prefer not."

It seemed clear that the rather foxy Gervase Henshaw had really more than suspected a studied game of bluff. But now Gifford's attitude tended to put that out of the question.

"In the circumstances, as your statement will consist mainly of a slander against me and my dead brother," Henshaw replied sullenly, "I prefer to keep out of the business for the present. I fancy," he added with an ugly significance, "that the police will be quite equal to dealing with the situation without any assistance or intervention from me."

Gifford ignored the covert threat. "Very well, then," he said, throwing open the door and standing aside for Henshaw to pass out; "I will go alone. Yes; it will be better."

But Henshaw did not move.

"I don't quite gather," he said in answer to Gifford's glance of inquiry, "exactly what your object is in taking this step."

"I should have thought—" Gifford began.

"Is it," Henshaw proceeded, falling back now to his ordinary lawyer-like tone—"is it merely to checkmate what you are pleased to call my designs upon Miss Morriston?"

"That will be a mere incidental result," Gifford answered, shutting the door and coming back into the room. "My object is to put it, at once and for all, out of your power to hold over Miss Morriston the threat that she is at any moment liable to be accused—by you of all people—of your brother's murder, and so suggest that she is in your power."

"Why do you say by me, of all people?"

"You who profess an affection for her."

"Your word profess scarcely does me justice, Mr. Gifford," Henshaw returned, drawing back his shut lips. "I had, and have, a very sincere affection for Edith Morriston, which, it seems, I am not to be allowed to declare or even have credit for. As a man of the world you can hardly pretend to be ignorant of what a man will do when his happiness is at stake. What he does under such a stress is no guide to his real feelings. But we need not labour that point. My affection, genuine or not, seems to

be in no fair way to be requited, and I had already made
up my mind to leave it at that. I have merely kept up the
game to this point out of curiosity to see how far your–
shall we say knight-errantry?–would lead you. I will now
relieve you from the necessity of going through an act of
Quixotic folly which would assuredly, sooner or later,
have unpleasant consequences for you."

So Gifford realized with a thrill of pleasure that he
had won. He felt that in much of his speech the man was
lying; that no consideration of mere unrequited affection
had induced him to abandon his design.

"I am glad to hear you have come to a sensible
conclusion," he said as coolly as the sense of triumph
would let him. "Whatever happened you could hardly
have expected your–plans to succeed."

"I don't know that," Henshaw retorted, with a touch of
a beaten man's malice. "Anyhow I have my own ideas on
the subject. But looking into the future with my brother's
blood between us I think it might have turned out a
hideous mistake."

"A safe conjecture," Gifford commented, between
indignation and amusement at the cool way the man was
now trying to save his face.

"Anyhow there's an end of it," Henshaw said with an
air and gesture of half scornfully dismissing the affair.
"And so I bid you good afternoon."

As he walked towards the door Gifford intercepted
him.

"Not quite so fast, Mr. Henshaw," he said resolutely.
"We can't leave the affair like this."

"What do you mean?" Henshaw ejaculated, with a look
which was half defiant, half apprehensive.

"You have heard my story," Gifford pursued with
steady decisiveness, "and have, I presume, accepted it."

"For what it is worth." The smart of defeat prompted
the futile reply.

"That won't do at all," Gifford returned with sternness. "You either accept the account I have just given you, or you do not."

There was something like murder in Henshaw's eyes as he replied, "This bullying attitude is what I might expect from you. To put an end, however, to this most unpleasant interview you may take it that I accept your statement."

"To the absolute exoneration of Miss Morriston?"

"Naturally."

"I must have your assurance in writing."

Henshaw fell back a step and for a moment showed signs of an uncompromising refusal. "You are going a little too far, Mr. Gifford," he said doggedly.

"Not at all," Gifford retorted. "It is imperatively necessary."

"Is it?" Henshaw sneered. "For what purpose?"

"For Miss Morriston's protection."

The sneer deepened. "I should have thought that purpose quite negligible, seeing how valiantly the lady is already protected. But I have no objection," he added in an offhand tone, "as you seem to distrust the lasting power of bluff, to give you an extra safeguard. Indeed I think it just as well, all things considered, that Miss Morriston should have it. Give me a pen and a sheet of paper." Henshaw's manner was now the quintessence of insolence, but Gifford could afford, although it cost him an effort, to ignore it. With the practised pen of a lawyer Henshaw quickly wrote down a short declaration, signing it with a flourish and then flicking it across the table to Gifford. "That should meet the case," he said, leaning back confidently and thrusting his hands into his pockets. Dealing with one who, like himself, was learned in the law he had, to save trouble, written a terse declaration which he knew should be quite acceptable. It simply stated that from certain facts which had come to his knowledge he was quite satisfied that his brother's death had been caused by an accident, and that no one was to blame for it, and he thereby undertook to make no future charge or imputation against any one, in connection therewith.

"Yes, that will do," Gifford answered curtly when he had read the few lines.

Henshaw rose with a rather mocking smile. "I congratulate you on your—luck, Mr. Gifford," he said with a studied emphasis, and so left the room.

27
GIFFORD'S REWARD

With the precious declaration in his pocket Gifford lost no time in going to Wynford Place. His light heart must have been reflected in his face, for Edith Morriston's anxious look brightened as she joined him in the drawing-room. All the same it seemed as though she almost feared to ask the result, and he was the first to speak.

"I bring you good news, Miss Morriston. You have nothing more to fear from Gervase Henshaw."

"Ah!" She caught her breath, and for a moment seemed unable to respond. "Tell me," she said at length, almost breathlessly.

"I have had a long and, as you may imagine, not very pleasant interview with the fellow," he answered quietly; "and am happy to say I won all along the line."

"You won? You mean–?"

He had taken the declaration from his pocket-book and for answer handed it to her. With a manifest effort to control her feelings she read it eagerly. Then her voice trembled as she spoke.

"Mr. Gifford, what can I say? I wish I knew how to thank you."

"Please don't try," he replied lightly. "If you only knew the pleasure it has given me to get the better of this fellow you would hardly consider thanks necessary. Would you care to hear a short account of what happened?" he added tactfully, with the intention, seeing how painful the revulsion was, of giving her time to recover from her agitation.

"Please; do tell me." She spoke mechanically, still hardly able to trust her voice above a whisper.

They sat down and he related the salient points of his interview with Henshaw. "It was lucky that I happened to have something of a hold over him," he concluded with a laugh; "Mr. Gervase Henshaw is not wanting in determination, and it took a long time to persuade him that he could not possibly win the game he was playing; but he stood to lose more heavily than he could afford. The conclusion, however, was at last borne in upon him that the position he had taken up was untenable, and that paper is the result."

"That paper," she said in a low voice, "means life to me instead of a living death; it means more than I can tell you, more than even you can understand."

He had risen, but before he could speak she had come to him and impulsively taken his hand. "Mr. Gifford," she said, "tell me how I can repay you."

Her eyes met his; they were full of gratitude and something more. But he resisted the temptation to answer her question in the way it was plain to him he was invited to do.

"It is reward enough for me to have served you," he responded steadily. "Seeing that chance gave me the power, I could do no less."

"You would have risked your life for mine," she persisted, her eyes still on him.

"Hardly that," he returned, with an effort to force a smile. "But had it been necessary, I should have been quite content to do so."

"And you will not tell me how I can show my gratitude?"

"I did not do it for reward," he murmured, scarcely able to restrain himself.

"I am sure of that," she assented. "But you once hinted, or at any rate led me to believe, that I could repay you."

There could be no pretence of ignoring her meaning now. Still he felt that chivalry forbade his acceptance.

"I was wrong," he replied with an effort, "and most unfair if I suggested a bargain."

"Have you repented the suggestion?" she asked almost quizzingly and with a curious absence of her characteristic pride.

"Only in a sense," he answered. "I hope I am too honourable to take an unfair advantage."

She laughed now; joyously, it seemed. "If your scruples are so strong there will be nothing for it but for me to throw away mine and offer myself to you."

"Edith," he exclaimed in a flash of rapture, then, checked the passionate impulse to take her in his arms. "You must not; not now, not now. It is not fair to yourself. At the moment of your release from this horrible danger you cannot be master of yourself. You must not mistake gratitude for love."

Edith drew back with a touch of resentful pride.

"If you think I don't know my own mind—" she began.

"Does anyone know his own mind at such a crisis as you have just passed through?" he said, a little wistfully. "Edith," he went on as he took her unresisting hand, "you must not be offended with me. Think. The whole object of what I have done for you has been to set you free, as free as though you had woke up to find the episode of these Henshaws had been no more than a horrible dream. You must be free; you must realize and enjoy your freedom. You are now relieved from the crushing weight you have borne so long; the release must be untouched by the shadow of a bargain expressed or implied. That is the only way in which a man of honour can regard the position."

"Very well," she returned simply, "I understand. I am sorry for my mistake."

Her manner shook his resolution. "I can't think you understand," he replied forcibly. "I only ask, in fairness to yourself, for time. Don't think that I am not desperately in love with you. You must have seen it, ever since our first confidential talk, that night at the Stograve dance. And my love has gone on increasing every day till–oh, you don't know how cruelly hard it is to resist taking you at your word. But I can't, I simply can't snatch at an unfair advantage, however great the temptation. I must give you time, time to know your own heart when the nightmare shall have passed away. I propose to return to town as soon as this man Henshaw has cleared out of the neighbourhood. Will you let us be as we are for a month, Edith, and if then you are of the same mind, send me a line and I will come to you by the first train. Is not that only fair?"

She gave a little sigh of contentment. "Very well," she said, "if that will satisfy you."

He took her hand. "It will seem a horribly long time to wait; but I feel it is right. Today is the 16th; on this day month I shall hear from you?"

"Yes, on the 16th," she answered.

"And so," he said, "you are free, unless you call me back to you."

"That is understood," she said with a smile.

He might have kissed her lips, her look into his eyes was almost an invitation, but, having steeled himself to be scrupulously fair, he refrained and contented himself with kissing her hand.

On reaching the hotel he heard with satisfaction that Henshaw had gone off by the late afternoon train and had suggested the unlikelihood of his returning. "So I suppose he is content to let the mystery remain a mystery," the landlord remarked. And the Coroner's jury subsequently had perforce to come to the same conclusion.

On the 16th of the following month, Hugh Gifford's impatience and anxiety were set at rest, as the morning's post brought the expected letter from Wynford.

"Dick and I are expecting you here tomorrow, unless you have changed your mind–I have not. The 3.15 train shall be met if you do not wire to the contrary."

When Gifford jumped out of the 3.15 Edith was on the platform. As they shook hands he read in her eyes an unwonted happiness and knew for certain that all was well.

"I had something to do in the town and thought I might as well come on to the station," Edith said with a lurking smile.

"I am glad you have not added even a half-hour to this long month," he replied as they took their seats in the carriage.

"It has been long," she murmured.

"Long enough to set our doubts at rest."

"I never had any," she replied quietly. He drew her to him and kissed her.

THE END

Resurrected Press Mysteries by J. S. Fletcher

The Orange-Yellow Diamond
When an elderly pawnbroker is murdered in the London parish of Paddington, a young, down on his luck writer is accused of the crime. But then it's found the pawnbroker had had in his possession an extraordinary South African diamond worth over eighty-thousand pounds — a diamond that's now missing. It falls to Melky Rubenstein to unravel the mystery and prove the young man's innocence.

The Middle Temple Murder
When an elderly man's body is found on the steps of chambers in the Midde Temple, one of the Inns of Court, it falls to newspaperman Frank Spargo and Detective-Sergeant Rathbury to solve the crime. The murdered man, for indeed it was murder, was found with no money or identification on his person except for a piece of paper with the name and address of a young barrister. Who is the victim? Why was he killed? Who is the murderer?

Scarhaven Keep
Bassett Oliver, the famed actor, has gone missing. When Oliver fails to show for a rehearsal, aspiring playwright Richard Copplestone finds himself sent to the small village of Scarhaven on the northern coast of England to track down the actors movements. What he finds is mystery. Find the answers as Copplestone unravels the mystery of Scarhaven Keep.

Visit www.resurrectedpress.com

Resurrected Press Mysteries by Fergus Hume

The Green Mummy

Professor Braddock hoped to compare the burial practices of the Egyptians with those of the ancient Peruvians with his latest acquisition, the mummy of the last Inca, Caxas. But on arrival, the packing case proved to hold not the mummy, but the body of his assistant Sidney Bolton. It falls to Archie Hope to discover the murderer if he is to marry the professors step-daughter, Lucy Kendal. Who killed Bolton and where is the mummy? Was it the sea captain Hervey? The mysterious Don Pedro? Cockatoo the Polynesian servant? The professor, himself? And what has become of the emeralds? These are the questions that Hope must answer amongst the secrets of the past in The Green Mummy.

The Mystery of a Hansom Cab

"Truth is said to be stranger than fiction, and certainly the extraordinary murder which took place in Melbourne Friday morning goes a long way towards verifying that saying." Thus opens The Mystery of a Hansom Cab, the best selling mystery of the nineteenth century. When a man is found dead in a hansom cab one of Melbourne's leading citizens is accused of the murder. He pleads his innocence, yet refuses to give an alibi. It falls to a determined lawyer and an intrepid detective to find the truth, revealing long kept secrets along the way. Fergus Hume's first and perhaps most famous mystery... The Mystery Of A Hansom Cab.

Visit www.resurrectedpress.com

Resurrected Press Mysteries from the Dr. John Thorndyke Series

Dr. John Thorndyke - Lecturer on Medical Jurisprudence and Forensic Medicine. Before Bones, before CSI, before Quincy, M.E – there was Dr. John Thorndyke solving the most baffling cases of Edwardian London using the latest tools of medical science. Read about his cases in:

The Eye of Osiris
John Bellingham, noted Egyptologist has vanished not once but twice in the same day. Now Dr, Thorndyke must unravel the tangled claims on his estate, solve the riddle of the missing man and find the "Eye of Osiris".

The Mystery of 31 New Inn
When Dr. Jervis is whisked away in a coach with no windows to an unknown location to treat a man in a coma from undivulged causes it is Dr. Thorndyke who must come up with the solution.

The Red Thumb Mark
The first of Dr. Thorndyke's cases finds him trying to prove the innocence of a young man accused of being a diamond thief despite the fact that his finger print was found at the scene of the crime.

John Thorndyke's Cases
More cases of medical mysteries as told by his trusted assistant Jervis, M.D. Eight stories of crime and deduction in Edwardian London.

Visit www.resurrectedpress.com

Resurrected Press Mysteries by John R. Watson & Arthur J. Rees

The Hampstead Mystery

High Court Justice Sir Horace Fewbanks found shot dead in his Hampstead home, a butler with a criminal past, a scorned lover and a hint of scandal. These are the elements of the Hampstead Mystery that Detective Inspector Chippenfield of Scotland Yard must unravel with the assistance of the ambitious Detective Rolfe. But will he be able to sort out the tangled threads of this case and arrest the culprit before he is upstaged by the celebrated gentleman detective Crewe. Follow the details of this amazing case at it plays out across Hampstead, London and Scotland until it reaches a stunning conclusion in the courts of the Old Bailey.

The Mystery of the Downs

When Harry Marsland was caught in a sudden down pour he sought shelter at Cliff Farm. Met at the door by a young woman clearly expecting someone else he is only too glad to get inside to wait out the storm. When they hear a noise upstairs in the deserted house they investigate only to discover the body of the farm's owner, Frank Lumsden, dead of a gunshot wound. Who then, killed Lumsden, and why? Who was the woman expecting and did she have any roll in the murder? These are the questions that private detective Crewe must answer in The Mystery of the Downs.

Visit www.resurrectedpress.com

Other Resurrected Press Mysteries

Mysteries on a Train

Before the Orient Express there was:

The Rome Express by Arthur Griffiths
A man is found dead in his first class sleeping compartment on the express from Rome to Paris. Who was his murderer? The Countess? The English General? His brother the clergy man? The maid who has disappeared? Is the French justice system up to solving the crime? Read about it in The Rome Express.

The Passenger from Calais by Arthur Griffiths
Colonel Basil Annesley finds he is the only passenger on the train from Calais to Lucerne. That is until a mysterious woman shows up at the last minute to book a compartment. Who is after her? What is her secret? Is she a criminal or a victim? Read about it in The Passenger from Calais

Visit us at www.resurrectedpress.com

About Resurrected Press

A division of Intrepid Ink, LLC, Resurrected Press is dedicated to bringing high quality, vintage books back into publication. See our entire catalogue and find out more at www.ResurrectedPress.com.

About Intrepid Ink, LLC

Intrepid Ink, LLC provides full publishing services to authors of fiction and non-fiction books, eBooks and websites. From editing to formatting, from publishing to marketing, Intrepid Ink gets your creative works into the hands of the people who want to read them. Find out more at www.IntrepidInk.com.